CHOOSING TO

Bloom

a novel by

Eugenie Davidsen

Cover designed by Jinny Nieviadomy, Artistic Incidents Studio
Author photo by Stephanie Harrington Photography
Back cover written by Amy Wilkinson
Technology support by Grayson Marsh

Produced by:

FriesenPress
Suite 300 – 852 Fort Street
Victoria, BC, Canada V8W 1H8

www.friesenpress.com

Distributed to the trade by The Ingram Book Company

"This book is dedicated to my entire family.
Each member has been an inspiration to me."

TABLE OF CONTENTS

Chapter 1

PICKING A PRETTY FLOWER

"Did you happen to notice the most gorgeous little lady standing over there in the far corner by the podium?" Sara asked her friend Meaghan. She turned towards the stage and tried not to point towards a very striking-looking, petite woman. Her shining dark blonde highlighted hair, cut in a shoulder-length bob, was the perfect cut for her, and her facial features were beautiful. Dressed in a tailored, deep-chocolate brown skirt suit with a burnt orange silk scarf woven around her neck, she looked absolutely stunning. Sara's gaze traveled down the little woman's body, and then on down her long, shapely legs and ankles, which led to tiny feet dressed in very high chocolate-brown alligator heels. "She is very attractive, but I was thinking more of that beautiful younger woman standing by the exit sign. Just look at that mass of hair," Meaghan exclaimed excitedly trying not to point to her subject.

This woman appeared to be in her early thirties, with a mass of curly burgundy/black hair hanging half-way down her back. Her makeup was applied very skillfully and truly was a work of art, making her complexion appear as soft and smooth as creamy silk. "She certainly is gorgeous, Meaghan, but don't you think we need to choose someone not quite so exotic? Someone a little more real, a person we can all relate to?" Sara asked.

Meaghan linked her arm through Sara's and suggested, "Let's take a stroll around the room and see if there are any other options. We need to find someone with a gorgeous figure, who can present herself well; she mustn't be afraid to speak in public. And Sara, of course she has to have a great personality. You know what I mean? We need a gal who can just charm the pants right off the audience." She giggled and added, "Pardon the expression."

Sara and Meaghan both belonged to the Enlighten Weight Loss Program, and strongly believed that this program was the perfect weight-loss plan. They had both lost a significant amount of weight, became more physically active, and been able to maintain their weight loss for more than a year. Many of the women belonging to the organization had been able to be taken off their medical prescriptions by their doctors, this certainly being an added bonus due to their lifestyle changes.

Sara was a close-to-sixty-year-old grandmother with a heavy chest and broad hips. Her layered, chin-length hair still retained its natural shade of white blonde with golden highlights. Sara's smile was contagious; her face free of the worry wrinkles that so often accompanied a woman of middle age. She glowed with an inner joy which radiated out to those around her. Tonight, Sara was wearing a linen skirt in a deep marine blue that was very softly gathered at the waist, along with a matching single-breasted blazer. Under this blazer she wore a gorgeous silk shirt in a deep magenta, and around her neck hung a sparkling gold chain which held a single solitary diamond. Her pierced ears each held a matching diamond glittering happily from the reflection in the overhead lights.

Meaghan and Sara were completely opposite in their outward appearance. Meaghan stood five feet six inches tall as compared to Sara's five feet and two inches. Meaghan's slimness made her appear even taller than she actually was. Adding to this was her three-inch stiletto black matte heels. Her luminous blue-black hair hung long and straight mid-way down her back. Meaghan was a natural beauty with creamy white skin and soft hazel-green eyes. She moved about the room with ease and grace. This night, she chose to wear a floor-length, jet black one-piece dress, with three-quarter-length flowing sleeves. The slim-fitting dress gathered at the waistline with a narrow silver belt accentuated Meaghan's tiny waist and her very long legs. Around Meaghan's neck she had loosely-twisted a variegated red silk scarf—the perfect touch to brighten up her dark ensemble. On her left wrist, Meaghan wore a wide silver bangle bracelet centered with a huge cut-glass emblem in the shape of a diamond; silver hoop earrings adorned her ears. Meaghan looked elegant.

"Well, you might be right, Sara," Meaghan said when they ended up on the opposite side of the room. "That little lady you pointed out is exuding charm, personality and poise; she definitely must be following our Weight Loss program to look that good. She's got my vote."

"Great! Now we have to find out if she's even interested in becoming our spokesperson for Enlighten," Sara said.

"Let's go ask her," Meaghan said with a mischievous smile.

"Do you think we should try and find out a little bit about her before we approach her?" Sara replied.

"Wonderful idea," said Meaghan. "Let's go see if we can find some information about her! Her name tag says 'Anna.'"

Meaghan and Sara walked over to the registration book and searched for Anna's name. "Anna Baldman lives in Loon Creek, Saskatchewan. This says she's fifty-four years old and has been an Enlighten member since 1991," Meaghan said.

"Wow! She's been an Enlighten weight-loss member forever. I bet she knows more about the program than we do—that's wonderful!" Sara said.

"This is so exciting!" Meaghan agreed, as she raised her hand to give Sara a high five. "Let's go ask her!"

The two friends made their way towards the group of women surrounding Anna. When Sara caught Anna's eye, she motioned her to come over.

"Anna, we've been watching you, and we have something to ask you; can you spare us a few minutes of your time?" Sara asked.

"Of course I can. Excuse me ladies, I'll be back," Anna said, flashing her companions a delightful smile.

Sara, Anna and Meaghan spied a secluded corner in the large banquet room and decided to go there. After

Sara and Meaghan introduced themselves to Anna they presented her with their request.

"Anna, you've probably heard rumors that Enlighten is searching for an ambassador to travel across Canada to promote their weight loss program." Sara said.

Anna slowly nodded her head up and down. "Yes, of course I have. I think it's a wonderful idea. A lot of women I know are really scared of getting into a weight-loss program. They think it's either just a money scam, or they'll have to live without all the delicious, comforting foods they enjoy."

"Well, Meaghan and I are impressed with your track record in the program, and both of us admire the way you look and present yourself. We've decided to ask you to consider being our candidate for Enlighten to represent Saskatchewan. Your beauty, along with your charming personality, is very endearing; we think you would be perfect for the position," Sara said.

"Who me, are you kidding?" Anna asked incredulously. "Take a look at all the loverly ladies in this room. There has got to be someone more suitable—there's no lack of gorgeous women here!"

Meaghan giggled and said, "'Loverly'—that's a *great* word. I must remember to use that one sometime."

In response to Meaghan's comment, Anna replied. "To me loverly means - not only beautiful on the outside but full of beauty on the inside as well."

"You're right Anna—there *are* a lot of gorgeous women here—but Meaghan and I do believe that *you're* our best choice. You can certainly take some time to think about it, but we're serious—we want *you*! As far as I know, there's no set itinerary for the trip yet, but if you decide to come on board, we'll contact the head office and find out all the details for you," Sara added giving Anna a huge smile.

"Tell us about yourself, Anna. Do you have any formal training in leadership or public speaking?" Meaghan asked.

"Yes, I have taken a few on line and mail order correspondence courses, just for my own benefit," Anna said. "I completed a course in writing children's stories, and also some public speaking classes. Is that important?"

"We believe it is, don't we, Meaghan? If you can form creative sentences and put them on paper, it should certainly help you form thoughts quickly when you're required to speak publicly and you don't have a script prepared. Of course, public speaking will be an essential part of your duties," Sara replied and then continued. "You would be competing against the chosen representatives from the nine other Canadian provinces and the three territories. There will be a panel of judges to decide who will be going forward in the competition," Sara said, slipping her arm around Anna's shoulders and giving her a gentle hug.

"As Sara mentioned, we believe that, altogether, there will be thirteen contestants chosen from across Canada, and we think that the competition will be in Edmonton, or Saskatoon, in early spring," said Meaghan. "Basically, all that's required of you at that point will be to present yourself to the best of your ability; you may be asked some specific questions about your home province, and possibly some questions about how the Enlighten Program has worked for you.

"There will be twelve honorary Weight Loss Members acting as judges, and they will decide which one of you will make the best ambassador. After some training, the chosen delegate will travel across Canada and speak at various locations representing our weight-loss program. Your duties will last for a year. Of course, there's only a few perks to the job: a new wardrobe, professionally-applied makeup, a gorgeous hairdo every day, and deportment training. From this exposure, you might even get agents from various products buzzing around you, requesting you to do television commercials or magazine ads. It could be the start of something huge for you! You could become our next super model!" Meaghan said, beaming as she talked. "It's a wonderful opportunity for anyone who has the time and doesn't mind the traveling," she continued. "Of course, you would be living out of a hotel room for a year, but there is a salary attached to this position; I'm not sure how much it is, and all your expenses and training will be provided for. Do you know any more details, Sara?"

"Wow! This is so out of my comfort zone!" said Anna. "I'm a very private person. Do I even want to be out there, exposing myself in front of all of Canada?" Anna paused as she pondered her options. "On the other hand," she continued, "it sounds so exciting—it's a chance not many people will get in their lifetime!"

"I'm sorry, I don't know any more details," Sara said in response, "but you think about this, honey, and let us know by the end of the week."

"Okay," Anna said, overcome with emotion. "I'll think it over, and once again, I don't know what to say. I'm so overwhelmed and honored that you would consider me for this position. Thank you for believing in me!" Tears were forming in Anna's eyes. She reached out and hugged Sara and then Meaghan. Then with a little smile, and in a stunned voice, she said, "Both of you are great. My husband won't believe this!"

She turned and walked back to the group she had been talking to, but she knew her evening was done. She was way too excited. Her mind was traveling in a dozen different directions at the same time. Anna offered apologies to her companions for leaving, said goodnight, and made her exit. She walked slowly out to the parking garage and found her three-year-old red mini-van. Digging around in her purse for her car keys, she finally found them and opened the hatchback. She swung her bags in, and climbed into the driver's seat.

Anna's small frame barely reached five feet tall. Because of her shortness, every extra ounce of weight seemed to show on her, and she had to work very hard to keep the weight down to her desired one hundred and five pounds. She decided to stop at a convenience store on her way out of the city and pick up a coffee to go. "I need some caffeine," she thought, "then I'll be ready to hit the road."

Chapter 2

INTRODUCING ANNA

Fifty-four years ago, Anna had been born into a "dirt poor" Saskatchewan farm family. Anna was the youngest of four girls. Her parents, young and in love, had migrated to Canada from Denmark as newlyweds when the Second World War was breaking out in their country. They had heard of homestead land available in northern Saskatchewan and decided to make the move. Once there, they tried to live out their idea of the Canadian dream. They believed that working hard, trusting in the good Lord, treating everyone with kindness and love (or as Anna's father frequently said, "Fairly and squarely") should enable them to live happily ever after!

But farm life in northern Saskatchewan was far more difficult than anyone could have imagined. The long, harsh winters with below-zero temperatures were tough on both man and beast alike. When the long-awaited summer season finally came, there was often too much rain, preventing the crops from being planted on time;

some years, there wouldn't be any rain at all for weeks on end, and then the already-planted crops weren't able to germinate. The Canadian dream didn't always end up the way it was envisioned! Many poor, disillusioned farmers headed back to the cities to find work that would provide them with a monthly paycheck, enabling them to feed their families.

Anna's mind wandered back to her childhood. She was born in 1958, when the majority of the population in Canada was struggling to get their lives back on track after the second world war. Anna's father had applied to join up with the army back in his home country, but was declined due to hearing impairment. For this Anna was exceptionally grateful and thanked God.

For the first couple of years in Canada, Hans and Inga Johannsenn, Anna's parents, hired themselves out as farm laborers wherever they could find work. No one had any money to pay them, so they were often given their wages in animals or garden vegetables.

Finally, the big day came when Hans felt it was time to file for their own homestead. Hand in hand, Hans and Inga set out walking to the nearest town and filed a claim for their chosen land. Between the two of them, they had managed to earn a fairly young Jersey milk cow, a few white laying hens, and a strutting red feathered rooster. Inga and Hans believed that God was totally responsible for their many blessings, and were grateful daily for their good health and abundant supply of strength.

An empty wooden grain bin became their first home. The one-room home was twelve feet wide by twelve feet long. This room served as a bedroom, kitchen, living room and a dining room. The bathroom was a two-seater outhouse, hidden behind a small grove of Blue Spruce trees in their backyard. In her much-valued free time, Inga spent many hours happily braiding faded rags into pretty scatter rugs that she used to cover the bare plank floors in the house.

There were no windows, very little insulation and the roof leaked when it rained, in their honeymoon home. The couple's main source of heat was an old pot-bellied wood-burning stove. When winter came, Hans hauled in a large empty fuel barrel that Inga scrubbed until it shone. This was filled with snow, which, when melted, became their water supply. Outside, Hans shoveled the heavy, white snow around the house, making it appear to be one huge snow bank. This proved to be a wonderful form of insulation, which helped to keep them warm and cozy in the below-freezing temperatures.

In summer, their water supply was pure, cold, refreshing water hauled in by pails from a well out by the barn; this well provided water for the family and the farm animals.

One year later, Anna's oldest sister, Abigail, was born in this tiny house, with the help of a midwife; eleven months later, sister number two, Libby, came into the world. Soon, number three—Danielle—joined the little family.

Three girls born in three years meant they were quickly outgrowing their little one-roomed home, but the family continued to live in this little dwelling for three more years, and then when the couple realized they would be blessed with child number four, Hans and Inga decided they had saved enough money to build a new house. This home, practically a mansion in the girls' eyes, had two bedrooms, a kitchen/dining room, a living room, and a porch. It was in this new house that Anna, the fourth daughter, was born, thus completing the Johannsenn family.

The Johannsenn's survived and thrived on mixed farming, which meant raising animals for their meat and for market, and planting grain crops and grass crops for selling and feeding the animals. This became the way of life for most families in Loon Creek.

Anna remembered fondly that about five miles from the Johannsenn home was a small community store/ post office. Dad (Hans) had been able to purchase an old 1954 Dodge Fargo half-ton truck from a neighbor and in his spare time, he tinkered on it, until he had it up and running. This was their mode of transportation when they traveled to the general store.

The four sisters took turns riding along. Their dad would only take two of the girls at a time, while the other two stayed home with their mother. Anna loved when it was her turn to go on the five-mile trip.

Rows and rows of wooden shelves hanging on the walls in the little storehouse were covered with brightly-colored cans and bottles. Stacks of beautiful fabrics in a multitude of textures and colors were huddled together on the bare plank floor in one corner of the market. These materials were Anna's favorite section of the store, and her imagination would run wild with fantasies of elegant gowns and special Sunday dresses and hats with feather plumage, like those she'd seen in the mail order catalogue. When Anna walked into the little store, she would breathe in deeply, filling her senses with the combined smells of raw leather, coal oil, soap and candles, and Anna wasn't sure what else.

The store owner, Mr. Andy, always let Anna and her sisters each choose one piece of hard candy to suck on as they browsed. This was always a difficult decision for Anna. Each little morsel of flavored sugar and coloring looked so desirable, she just wanted to sit and look and smell them. Often she would take too long, and her sister would jab her in the ribs and hiss "hurry up." At that point, Anna would shut her eyes tightly and quickly grab one; she never found one she didn't like.

Back on the farm, Inga Johannsenn insisted on planting a huge vegetable garden each spring. Of course, the entire Johannsenn family was required to help pull the weeds, harvest the vegetables, and preserve food for the winter months.

The four girls were taught at a young age which wild berries were edible and where to find them. Come spring they were sent out almost daily to the hilly green pastures or deep dark dense woodlands to pick the wild berries. Sometime later, the four girls would come trudging home, pails laden with the ripe, sweet-smelling fruit which their mother magically made into jams, jellies, and fruit pies.

Anna was a happy child, but because she was four years younger than her third sister, she was considered by her sisters to be a baby, and was therefore left on her own to play by herself. However, Anna had a great imagination, and invented games and treasure hunts to keep herself busy.

Mom and Dad Johannsenn were excellent providers, and there was always enough food on the table—most times *too* much. Anna was told many times by her dad to eat until it hurt, so she did. Anna thought this was probably the beginning of her weight problem.

When the Johannsenn children turned six, they were required to walk a mile and a half to a one-room school-house. In the winter months, their dad hooked up a little one-horse sleigh called a cutter, and drove the girls to school in this. Piled into the cutter amid blankets and school books and lunch pails—Anna thought this was the best! None of her school friends had such a fanciful mode of transportation. By the time Anna started grade one, her oldest sister, Abby, was old enough and strong enough to drive a horse and cutter to school. The horse would spend the day in a stable by the schoolhouse and was fed hay brought along from home.

Students at this country school weren't plenti-ful. Often children were kept at home to help their parents with the farm work, so attendance was sporadic depending on the farming season. Anna remembers about a dozen students in various grades, all with the same teacher. Qualified teachers were in big demand and hard to get to a remote country school. Most often the teacher was a past student who had finished grade twelve. Anna's dad was a school board trustee, and often provided the teacher, always a female, with room and board. This meant that the four girls had to give up their precious bedroom and were required to sleep together on the floor in the living room. However, the added income did supply a few store-bought necessities.

Anna and her sisters were also required to help their dad care for the farm animals. Anna didn't have much liking for the noisy, smelly pigs. They were always squealing for no reason at all—at least that Anna could see.

The one milk cow they had started with was good at birthing heifer calves, providing the family with a half-dozen milk cows. These massive creatures scared Anna. Sometimes they would walk right up behind her and give her a shove with their soft, wet, velvet noses. Anna knew that they wouldn't bite her, but she was afraid of getting stepped on by their big, clumsy feet.

When Anna was about four years old, a kind old neighbor brought her a soft, cuddly, orphaned lamb. Anna thought he was the best pet ever; she fed him cow's milk from an old baby bottle and named him Tommy. Following her everywhere, he became her shadow. Tommy would listen to her stories, and he never talked back or called her a baby like her sisters did. His soft little body was covered in a curly coat of pure white wool, into which Anna loved to bury her face and bare arms. His wet nose, pointy little ears, stubby pompom tail and all four of his boots were velvety smooth and black.

As Tommy grew older, he became very frisky and quite rough. He wouldn't listen to Anna or her father. It was the girl's job to go out to the backyard and collect firewood to burn in the kitchen stove. Just as the firewood carrier bent over to pick up a piece of wood, Tommy would charge up behind, ram his head into her backside and send her sprawling and bawling all at the same time. No amount of scolding by Anna or her father would make him stop this bad habit. So one day, Tommy just disappeared. Anna was heartbroken.

Anna also loved her dad's two big old work horses; one was named Dolly and the other Nelly. Each of them wore a soft deep chestnut brown coat, and they had matching white stars on their foreheads. Their big stomping feet were covered in long shaggy white hair, making them look like they were wearing slouching white socks. Anna remembered spending many moments sitting on the rail fence watching them throw back their heads and race around the corral. They seemed to have a sense of freedom when they did this which made Anna think, *they must be pretending they're wild stallions.*

Other inhabitants on the Johannsenn farm were some messy, sassy chickens which roamed the grounds freely. Anna remembered that she would often step into a pile of chicken poo in her bare feet, which disgusted her to no end. Then she would run as fast as she could to some fresh clean green grass, and rub and rub until her foot was clean.

As the girls grew older it became Abby and Libby's job to milk the cows. These two girls were inseparable, like Siamese twins. Whenever their mom or dad called for one of the girls, they both appeared. Abby's coloring was the same as her dad's: pitch-black hair, sky-blue eyes and her pretty little face was covered in freckles. Libby's hair was dark brown, her eyes were a beautiful hazel-green, and her face was freckle-free. The two girls (being only eleven months apart) were the same size, and Mrs. Johannsenn often sewed them matching dresses.

Danielle, the third daughter, was born a feisty little curly-haired redhead with a red hot temper to match, bright blue eyes and a very pale complexion, covered in maroon freckles. While the fourth daughter, Anna, was blessed with poker straight golden-blonde hair, deep chocolate brown eyes, like her mother's and skin that turned brown from the sunshine.

Unlike Libby and Abby, Danielle and Anna did not get along with each other. Anna felt that Danielle was continually criticizing her and finding fault with everything she tried to do. It seemed to Anna that Danielle was always ready to run and tattletale to their parents. Anna soon became aware of Danielle's tactics, and tried to avoid that sister as much as possible.

Danielle and Anna were responsible for feeding the chickens and collecting their eggs. Anna didn't like the chickens very much, but they were better than the cows. The chickens were smelly and messy and noisy, but at least they wouldn't hurt her if they stepped on her toes—and besides, she thought, *they're chicken, right?* Then she would run and give them a little chase, which sent them flying in all directions.

Sunday was a day of rest for the Johannsenn family. On that day, the whole family would pile into a much bigger sleigh (in winter) or wagon (in summer) and head off to the schoolhouse to attend church service. There was no church building, and there was not always a qualified minister available, so often the service was put together by members of the community. Of course, not all the local families attended church, but Anna grew up believing in one God, who was the Father, the Son, Jesus Christ and the Holy Spirit. She believed that Jesus Christ died on the cross to atone for her sins and then three days later rose again leading the way to eternal life for anyone who believed.

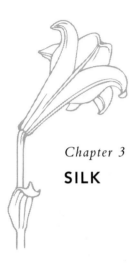

Chapter 3

SILK

Anna's mind snapped back to the present and came to rest on her sister Danielle. As much as the two girls had quarreled and tried to outdo each other as children, Anna felt like they were becoming friends at last. *I guess sometimes friendship can take years to develop*, she thought. Anna felt happy that she and her sister were finally learning to love and accept each other.

Anna glanced at the speedometer. She was traveling north along the highway at one hundred kilometers an hour in her little red mini-van. She would be home soon.

What am I doing? She thought. *Little women from Loon Creek don't get to travel across Canada as an ambassador for a weight-loss program. Are you crazy, Anna?* She scolded herself. *What will your husband think?*

He'll think you've lost your marbles, that's what he'll think! Anna answered herself.

What about my children and grandchildren? She continued to think. *Nothing is as important to me as God and my family and our privacy. Will my publicity have any negative impact on them? Do I really want to be in the spotlight? I need to give this some serious thought and prayer.*

Anna proceeded to pray silently for the rest of the drive home. Soon she was pulling into her driveway; reaching up, she pressed the remote-control button on her sun visor, opening the garage door. Once inside, Anna gathered up her belongings, pulled the keys out of the ignition, and headed inside the house. She was tired and let out a big sigh. "Hello?" she called as she walked in the door.

No answer.

She put down her overnight case and purse, and walked into the kitchen. She called out again, "Silk, are you home?" She plugged in the electric kettle, and proceeded to put away her belongings. The water boiled, and she made herself a cup of hot lemon tea.

A red light was blinking on the message machine and Anna pressed it. The message was from her daughter, Cindy.

"Hi Mom, just wanted to see if you're home yet. Give me a call when you get in. We're all fine. Love you. Bye."

Anna sat down and sipped her tea. She'd call Cindy later; first she wanted to talk to her husband, Silk. She heard the front door open, and Silk called out, "Hi honey, I'm home!"

"I'm home, too. I missed you!" Anna called back, standing to greet him.

"How was your meeting? Were the roads good?" he asked as he appeared in the kitchen. He wrapped his arms around his wife. "Umm, you smell good," he said.

Anna returned his hug. "The meeting was excellent, and the roads were clear, and I have lots to tell you. But first tell me about your weekend." Anna requested, pushing herself back and looking up into Silk's handsome face.

"Well, it was pretty quiet around here, with you gone, so I called Rod and we went out for a ride on our quads," Silk replied. "We rode out to the Waterhen Lake, had lunch there, swung around by Meadow Creek and then came on home. It was a good day for riding."

"Well, good for you. That does sound like a nice ride. Your machine was working well? No problems?" Anna asked.

"It was working great. We enjoyed being out in the fresh air and sunshine." He pulled up a kitchen chair and sat down at the table. "Now tell me about your meeting."

"You're never going to believe what they want me to do!" Anna exclaimed.

"Who wants you to do what?" Silk asked, calmly looking over at his wife.

"I've been chosen by the Saskatchewan committee for Enlighten Weight Loss to represent this province as Enlighten's Canadian Ambassador. Can you believe it?" Anna asked excitedly.

"Tell me all about it," Silk said.

Anna told Silk everything she knew about the proposal.

"Well, it certainly sounds like an exciting opportunity. Is this something you think you'd like to do?" he asked her.

"I don't know yet," Anna responded. "I'd get to travel all across Canada, at the company's expense. I would get complete makeovers and new clothes and my hair styled professionally everyday. What woman wouldn't love that?" She paused, and continued. "You know how much I believe that maintaining a healthy body weight is very important, and I do trust this program for being the best available option for doing that, so it wouldn't be a hardship to promote it…I just don't know if I can be who they want me to be," Anna added sounding doubtful.

"Anna, you just have to be yourself! They don't want you to be anybody else. You were chosen because they like exactly who you are." Silk said. "You know, I was just reading an article today that said, 'The key to success is self-confidence, and the key to self-confidence is being prepared.' We all know that no one is more prepared than you."

"I try to be, and I know you're right; that's good advice, but I feel so inadequate. I'm finding it really hard to wrap my head around this."

"Well, just take your time and think about it. I know you'd do a great job, if you decide to go for it!" Silk said.

Anna smiled at her husband and went over to give him another hug. He was definitely her biggest fan and she did love him a lot. "You are good to me. Thanks for all your confidence in me, but I do need some time to think and pray about this. They've given me until Friday to decide," she said.

Silk walked to the cupboard, refilled the electric kettle with water from the tap, and plugged it in. "Well, honey, for what's it's worth," he said, as he sat down next to his wife, "You know I don't like it when you're away for long stretches of time without me, but hey, maybe I could fly out and join you when you get a day off. We could tour some cities we've never seen before, make it an adventure, what do you think of that?" Silk asked, smiling, and giving his wife a beguiling wink.

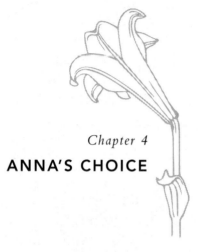

Chapter 4

ANNA'S CHOICE

Anna awoke early Friday morning with one purpose in mind. She picked up the phone and quickly dialled the phone number that appeared on a little blue business card sitting on her bedside table. Today was the deadline to let her name stand for the Enlighten Weight Loss Competition and she was overflowing with excitement!

"Hello, Sara?" she asked when the phone was answered.

"Yes, this is Sara."

"Sara, its Anna, and I've reached my decision about your Enlighten proposal—but believe me; it's been a real roller coaster ride this past week! One minute I think there's no way I can do this, and that I'm not qualified, and then I think, yes, I want to do this, I *can* do this!"

"So what did you finally come up with? I can hardly wait for your answer, and I hope it's a yes!" Sara exclaimed.

"Sara, if you and Meaghan truly believe that I'm the right person for this job, then I'm throwing my name into the hat for this competition." Anna replied.

Sara squealed, "Oh Anna, I'm so glad, I know you'll do a wonderful job as the Saskatchewan representative, but remember, this is just the first step. You'll be competing against twelve other contestants from the other Canadian provinces and territories."

"Yes, of course, I know that Sara—the battle has just begun, so they say! But I'm up for the challenge," Anna said. She sang out in a happy voice, "Whatever will be, will be!"

"I'm thrilled for you, Anna; I know you're going to do a great job! You'll be the brightest star in the competition, outshining the other contestants by a mile."

"I wish I had your confidence, Sara. You know I'll do my best, and we'll see what happens." Anna assured her friend.

"I'm going to give Meaghan a call and tell her the good news. She'll be thrilled! Then I'll email head office and submit your name," Sara said. "You know that the deadline for all contestants is today, so by Monday we should get our instructions as to what the next step will be. Do you think you can wait that long?" Sara asked Anna.

"I guess I'll have to be okay with that, but now that I've made my decision, I'm excited to get going. We'll just wait and see what we have to do on Monday." Anna responded.

The ladies wished each other a great weekend, said their goodbyes and hung up their phones.

After clicking off the phone connection with Anna, Sara quickly dialled Meaghan's number and told her the good news. Megan let out a giant "WHOO, HOO!" and Sara quickly pulled the phone away from her ear. The two ladies congratulated each other on finding the perfect candidate and exchanged goodbyes.

Sara turned on her laptop computer and quickly typed a short email to the Enlighten head office informing them that Anna Baldman was their chosen representative for Saskatchewan. She proofread it for a second time and pressed the send button.

There, Sara thought. *It's official.* She signed out of her computer and started rubbing her hand. The middle finger on her right hand was swollen and she couldn't straighten it. Her right shoulder had been bothering her as well. *What's going on with this?* she thought. *I should make an appointment to see Dr. Dekker, but maybe it's just old age catching up with me.*

Sara went into the bathroom and popped two light blue pain pills into her mouth. She turned to go into her bedroom and get dressed when the front doorbell rang. *Now who could that be, so early in the morning?* Sara wondered as she hurried to answer it. Opening the door, she looked right into a broad chest of a man. Raising her head and looking up she realized it was her son, Luc; she let out a little squeal of delight.

"Luc, what are you doing here?" Reaching up, she wrapped her pajama-clad arms around his neck. "Come in, my boy!"

"Hi Mom, I have a few days off, and I couldn't think of anywhere else I'd rather be than right here with you!"

he said with a smile. "So here I am! I hope you're not too busy for the next couple of days."

"I've always got time for you, my son, you know that. I'm thrilled that you've come."

"I really need some R and R," Luc said, "but tell me what's new with you, Mom. You look great, by the way. What have you been up to?"

"What a flatterer you are, Luc—but come here—I need another big ole bear hug. Can I make you a cup of coffee or some breakfast, what would you like?" Sara asked, beaming from ear to ear.

Luc took a step towards Sara and gave her the requested hug. "Mmm, you smell good, Mom. Yes, I'm starving, but you go ahead and get what you want to eat. I can help myself. If you don't mind, I'll just check out your refrigerator. I know you always have great leftovers in there." Luc strolled over to the refrigerator opened the door and pulled out a can of cola. He lifted it up to show his mom and said, "I think I'll have this instead of coffee, if that's alright with you?" Sara glanced up at Luc and plugged in the electric kettle to make herself a cup of hot tea. She grabbed a teabag out of a hand-painted glass canister and dropped it into a delicate, fine china teacup, then she waited for the water to boil.

"You're welcome to have whatever you can find, Luc," she said. She prepared her tea with a bit of honey and a squeeze of fresh lemon. Carefully carrying the dainty china teacup full of tea to the kitchen table, she sat down and waited for her son to join her.

"Now about what's new in my life?" she said. "Well, not much, Luc—you know my days are mostly the same old routine. I'm sure your life is much more exciting than mine. Tell me what's been keeping you busy. How's work? Are you still seeing Lisa?"

"Work's really good, Mom, but I'm not sure about Lisa. That's one thing I need to talk to you about." Luc said with a frown. "But not right now; let's just relax and enjoy each other's company. I'm not ready to talk about that yet. I need to sort out a few things in my mind first."

"If you think that's best, Luc, then tell me all about your work. Have you flown to any exotic countries lately?" Sara asked.

"I really like my job and it's keeping me very busy. I flew to Vancouver this past week; in fact, the airline has offered me a new opportunity for the next year. If I want the job, which I think I do, I'll be flying round-trips from Saskatoon to Vancouver daily."

Luc had five years commercial pilot experience under his belt with the Canadian Airline Company. He was twenty-nine years old and couldn't think of anything he would rather be doing.

"That sounds wonderful, Luc. Maybe I'll get to see you more often, if your flights are all right here in Canada." Sara smiled and continued. "Congratulations, Luc!"

"Thanks, Mom, but I haven't accepted their offer yet. Now tell me what you've been up to?" Luc asked. "You know that I worry about you being alone too much, now that Dad's gone."

Luc's dad had passed away eighteen months previously after a short struggle with pancreatic cancer, and Luc still had a hard time believing he was gone, especially when he was here, in this house. He expected his dad to walk into the room at any minute. Sara reassured him. "It's getting easier to be alone. Of course, I still miss your father every day, but I get out with my lady friends, and I'm quite busy with the Enlighten Weight Loss program. You know that I'm one of the leaders for Enlighten in this area?"

"Good for you, Mom! Do you have any trips or vacations planned?" Luc asked.

"No, I'm not thinking that far ahead yet, but I might hear of something that interests me, if the price is right!" Sara replied with a smile.

"And what about Jaycee and Larry, what are they up to? I haven't heard from them for ages. I know it's probably my fault." Luc said. "I'm not real good at answering their emails or phoning them."

"Your sister and brother are doing fine, as far as I know. I talk to Jaycee almost daily. Larry and his little family are doing well too; everyone has such a busy life. Sometimes I wonder why we make ourselves so busy. When God looks down from Heaven we must look like tiny little ants scurrying around trying to get things done." Sara said wistfully. Jaycee, Sara's oldest child and only daughter, lived with her husband Chad, and were the proud parents of three-year-old twin boys named Solomon and Samuel. Their nicknames were Sol and Sammy, and of course Sara adored them. Next in the family came Luc, still single, and then the youngest son, Larry, who had married his childhood sweetheart, Nicole, at the age of twenty. Now five years later they had become the proud parents of a brand new baby girl named Sierra Jane.

Sara and her son spent the rest of the day relaxing and sharing tidbits of news about people in their lives and enjoying each other's company. Occasionally Luc would get up and rummage through the fridge looking for something to eat. When he found what he wanted, he would either heat it in the microwave or eat it cold. "Mom, your leftovers are the best. What is this, chocolate cake?" he asked, holding up a plastic-wrapped treasure.

Sara replied, "Yes, it is chocolate cake, with a low-cal raspberry cream filling. Is there enough left for both of us? I love that chocolate cake."

Luc shared the cake with his mother and they sat back and quietly enjoyed the sweet treat. When nine o'clock rolled around, Luc announced, "This has been a great day, Mom, but I'm bushed. I need some sleep. We have another day tomorrow, so I'll say good night. Thank you for being the same great, caring, mother that you always are. I love you." Luc leaned over and kissed his mother on the cheek, and then he headed off to his old bedroom.

Sara let out a long contented sigh and thought, *something is troubling that boy. His brow is covered in worry lines..* She tidied up the kitchen, putting the dirty dishes in the dishwasher, turned off all the lights, locked the front door, and headed up the stairs to her own bed.

The next day began with an overcast sky. Luc woke up early and quietly crept outside to wait for the sun to come up. Sometime later, Sara woke up and found him sitting outside on the back porch swing.

"What's up Luc? What's on your mind? A mother knows when something is troubling her child, even if he is all grown up."

"Mom, I'm really sorry to have to tell you this, but I think I've messed up big time." Luc said cautiously.

"You remember Lisa, the girl I was dating? Well, this is no excuse, but she told me she was taking birth control precautions, so I didn't. Anyway, long story short, she called me three weeks ago to tell me she's pregnant! She was not a happy camper! I told her it would be okay and that I was thrilled we were having a baby, and I asked her to marry me."

"Luc, congratulations!" Sara shouted joyously.

"Whoa, not so fast, Mom. Lisa told me that getting married was the last thing she wanted to do and that there's no way she's having a baby and she planned on getting rid of it as soon as possible! I begged her not to; I told her that if she had the baby I would gladly take it and raise it. She said she couldn't stand the thought of being pregnant. How could I have misjudged her so badly?" Luc wailed. "Mom, what can I do?"

"That's a very good question, son. What have you been doing for the last three weeks?" Sara asked.

"Mostly trying to find her and talk to her, but she's not responding. In between my airline flights I phone her constantly. What else can I do?"

"Well first of all, Luc, we both know that you've been raised to realize that babies are a wonderful gift from God—they are not a mistake. People make mistakes, but God never does. I truly believe that if Lisa chooses to end this baby's life, she's making a very grave error, one that she will regret for the rest of her life."

"I feel the same way, Mom, but she won't listen to me, and now she's not returning my calls," Luc groaned.

"Let's pray about this, Luc," Sara suggested.

"Mom, I'm not real big on prayer, but you go ahead."

Sara did. She reached out and put her hand on top of Luc's. Then she bowed her head and solemnly asked God to be with Lisa and Luc. She prayed that God would soften Lisa's heart and fill it with love towards the little unborn child. That God would give Lisa peace about being pregnant, and that Luc would receive the peace of mind that comes only from God, no matter what Lisa's decision would be. She asked this solemnly in Jesus Christ's name.

Chapter 5

SPROUTING

Monday morning dawned clear and sunny. Anna awoke, and stretched her arms up over her head. A soft smile played on her lips as she gazed at her husband Silk, still sound asleep beside her. Her body trembled with excitement. At this stage in Anna's life, one day was pretty much the same as the next, so Anna was thrilled that she'd signed up for the Enlighten competition.

I hope Sara calls me about it the minute she finds out any news. Anna thought. *I'm anxious to know who the other contestants are and when the whole process will begin. I wonder what the judges are looking for—youth, beauty, poise, maybe all three. Oh well, I'll do my best and try to have a little fun while I'm at it. I don't have anything to lose either way. Hopefully it will be a good experience.*

She started her fifteen-minute stretching routine, which she did first thing every morning. It seemed to help limber up her aging muscles for her daily activities. When she finished this, she walked into the kitchen, and filled the electric kettle with water. Most mornings, Anna started her day by drinking a cup full of steaming hot green tea, then she would prepare herself a small bowl of cooked oatmeal, which she ate with chopped up sections of orange or other fruit. She carried her tray into the dining room, bowed her head, and gave thanks to God for her meal. Anna continued to pray silently for her family while she was eating. Her usual prayer was thanking God for the health of her children and grand-children, and for their protection and safety. Whenever God planted certain issues on Anna's mind, she would pray for that. She always tried to be open to hearing God's voice..

Anna once heard a story about a man who had died; his soul went up to heaven. When he arrived in heaven, St. Peter showed him into a large storage room full of shelves holding rows and rows of beautifully-wrapped, unopened gifts. The man asked St. Peter who the gifts were for and why they weren't opened. St. Peter replied that these gifts were prayers that no one had asked for—so they just sat there unopened and unused. Anna remembered thinking, *what a shame that no one has asked God for these gifts,* so she was trying her best to ask God for the many blessings/gifts that were available to her and her family.

Anna jumped when the phone rang. She reached over and picked up the receiver. "Hello, Anna here!" she said.

"Hey Anna, it's me, Sara. I just got a call from the Enlighten Head office. Congratulations! You're in. I gave them your email address, and they should be emailing both of us a copy of the program later today. It looks like you'll be traveling to Saskatoon next week. Two other contestants, one from Alberta and one from British Columbia, will meet with us there. That should give us a sneak peek of what the competition looks like."

"Oh Sara, I'm so excited, I could scream! Thanks for calling me so early. Do you have any idea which day of the week they'll want me to come into the city? Do you know what this meeting will be all about, besides meeting the two other contestants?" asked Anna.

"I think there might be some training seminars. I read somewhere that there's one on dressing tips— 'Learning How to Dress to Look Ten Years Younger and Ten Pounds Lighter,' for example—as well as teaching techniques for applying makeup and hair artistry," Sara said.

"Well, that all sounds mighty interesting to me! I can hardly wait to learn all these special tips and techniques," Anna replied.

"Good for you, Anna. That's all I know for now. You have a great day, and I'll call you later when we get more details." Sara said, and signed off.

Anna hung up the phone and went back to sipping her tea. When she finished her tea, she stood up and began gathering her breakfast dishes together. Suddenly from nowhere, loving hands began caressing her shoulders. Strong fingers gently stroked her neck and slowly worked their way up to massage her temples.

Anna relaxed, sat back down, and let out a sigh of contentment. Silk continued gently massaging Anna's scalp and neck until she stood up, turned around, and pressed her body close to her husband's. Reaching up, she slipped her arms around his neck and ran her fingers through his hair.

"I think you should come back to bed for a while, honey. Aren't you still a little bit tired?" Silk whispered in a husky voice.

"All of a sudden I do feel very tired," Anna murmured. Anna and Silk walked arm and arm back to their bedroom.

Chapter 6

INTRODUCING MEGAN

For thirty years—which was Meaghan Marshall's entire life—she had lived in Saskatoon, Saskatchewan. Meaghan felt that her daughter Tara, now five years old, and son Cohen, almost three, were her heart and soul. Meaghan's mind wandered back to what her world had been like before her divorce. She had married her high school sweetheart, Marty Summers, when they were both fresh out of high school and nineteen years old. The marriage lasted only three years and then ended tragically—for Meaghan. Her heart was broken. She had tried in vain to get Marty to take counselling with her. She had been willing to try anything to make it work, but she couldn't do it on her own. The marriage had begun with passion and commitment, but for some reason unbeknownst to Meaghan, Marty lost interest in her.

How can a person change so much? Meaghan wondered. When they were dating, their friends considered them the "golden couple." Everyone thought their match was made in heaven. Physically, they looked good together. Meaghan was tall and slim with beautiful, long, black shining hair and sparkling green eyes. Her skin glowed with health and she retained a deep dark tan all year round. Marty, on the other hand, while being the same height as Meaghan, was very muscular and slim, with bleached platinum blonde hair and deep blue eyes. His occupation as a construction worker kept him lean and muscular. They not only looked good together, but they had fun together too. Their friends adored them as a couple.

It had bothered Meaghan slightly that, while they were dating, they didn't seem to have much in common. Meaghan liked to dance, play board games or sit quietly and read. Marty, on the other hand, loved making noise, the more the better. Riding around on his motor bike or revving up his souped-up cars were his passions. On Sundays, he'd often go out in the woods and take target practice with his array of guns. The sudden, harsh crack of the guns scared Meaghan.

But both of them liked to play pool and party with their friends. Marty and Meaghan were in love, and love conquers all, right? The couple got married and Meaghan quickly became pregnant. She stopped drinking and partying, but Marty didn't. Meaghan started growing up and being responsible for her actions. Marty didn't. As the months went by, there were definitely some good times. Beautiful daughter Tara was born, bringing much joy to Meaghan's life; Meaghan blossomed with motherhood. Marty continued to go out at night with his friends. When he did come home, long after Meaghan and Tara were in bed, he blamed her for not going out with him. He accused her of being unfaithful—apparently his drinking buddies had filled his head with all kinds of wild tales about her...or was it just Marty's alcohol-induced mind that made up these stories? Meaghan wasn't sure.

Meaghan remembered the night vividly when Marty had accused her of being with one of his friends before they were married. Meaghan vehemently denied ever being with anyone but him. Marty simply looked her in the eye and slapped her hard across the face. Meaghan never argued with Marty again! She became wary, realizing that when Marty was drinking, he was like a ticking time bomb, ready to go off at any second.

A few months later, Meaghan brought home a "home pregnancy test" which confirmed her suspicions that she was pregnant with their second child. She decided she would wait to tell Marty. Marty continued to stay out late and come home drunk. He made no excuses and didn't seem to care.

Meaghan started eating. She cooked and she ate. Her daughter and her food were her comfort. Often in the evenings, after putting Tara to bed, she would pull her cookbooks out of the cupboard and experiment with new recipes. Meaghan soon became lost in her passion for cooking, forgetting her loneliness. Her problems disappeared. She cut herself off from her friends and family. If no-one knew how unhappy she was, it didn't seem quite so real.

Eventually, Meaghan came to the realization that she couldn't keep on living like she was. She decided that it was time to take control of the situation. Valentine's Day was quickly approaching. Meaghan made a date with Marty for February fourteenth.

Valentine's Day is for lovers, right? She thought. *It will be a perfect time to tell him about the new baby and hopefully make a fresh start.*

Meaghan made a dinner reservation at the Hot Tamale Restaurant; she knew that Marty loved the food there. When they were dating, it had been one of their favourite hangouts. In the meantime, Meaghan joined the Enlighten Weight Loss Program and began following a healthy eating plan. She realized that her eating habits were way out of control and she felt like she was gaining weight by the minute. *It's no wonder Marty doesn't find me attractive any more!* She thought.

Finally, February fourteenth arrived. Tonight was date night, and Meaghan was all set to tell Marty about the new baby. Meaghan spent the entire afternoon pampering herself with a manicure and pedicure. While Tara was napping, Meaghan soaked in a hot fragrant bubble bath. She styled her hair and began searching for suitable clothing for the evening. Nothing fit! But Meaghan was determined not to let anything spoil her evening. She wanted to look as beautiful as she could. She settled on a black, a-line skirt. It was snug, but it was okay. She accessorized with some black hose and shiny black pumps.

A nice red shirt would be perfect, but I don't have one, Meaghan thought.

Meahgan reached for the phone and called her sister, Hattie. Hattie had great clothes, and the sisters were about the same size. *Maybe I can borrow a shirt from Hattie,* Meaghan reasoned.

"Hello, Hattie. How are you?" Meaghan asked when the phone was answered.

"Oh, hi, is this Meaghan?" Hattie inquired. "What have you been up to? It's been ages since I've heard from you."

"I know…life just gets too busy, Hattie, but honey, I have a date with Marty this evening, and I need to borrow a shirt from you, hopefully in red. Do you have something that would work that I could borrow?" Meaghan asked hopefully.

"I do, actually. I'll get it ready for you. Where are you going?" Hattie asked.

"I made reservations at the 'Hot Tamale' which is only a couple of blocks from your house. Will it be all right if we just stop on our way to the restaurant and get it?"

"Sure, that works for me. We'll be home. I'll get a couple of other shirts ready for you too, and then you can choose which one you like!"

"Oh, thanks, Hattie. You are a lifesaver. Our reservation is for seven o'clock, so we should be there about six forty five. Oh, I hear Tara fussing, I have to go. Thanks again. I'll see you later." Meaghan said quickly and hung up the phone.

She made her way to the nursery to get her daughter. Tara was standing up in the crib, calling for her mother; when she saw her, she reached out her arms to be picked up.

"There's my big girl, did you have a good sleep? Momma loves you." Meaghan cooed to her daughter. She picked Tara out of her bed and carried her over to the rocking chair. They sat down and cuddled.

Tara said "Bibbs?" in her sweet little-girl voice.

"Snowball isn't here right now. I don't know where she is," Meaghan replied. A few days earlier, Meaghan had found a dirty, scrawny, little grey kitten outside and had taken her in. After Meaghan had fed the little orphan and got the dirt and matted hair cleaned up, she realized that the kitten had beautiful, soft, pure white fur. "Snowball is the perfect name for you." She told the kitten. Of course Tara loved the little ball of fluff and couldn't keep her hands off her but for some reason known only to Tara, she insisted on calling the little pet Bibbs.

"You must be getting hungry, my girl. Let's take you to the pottie and then Momma will find you some supper."

Meaghan proceeded to take Tara to the toilet and then after washing their hands carried her into the kitchen. "What are you hungry for today, my girl?" Meaghan asked her daughter. She set Tara on the floor and placed a wicker basket full of toys next to her. Tara happily emptied the toys from the basket, one by one by one.

When Meaghan had finished preparing Tara's meal of strained sweet potatoes and green beans, she set her in her high chair. Tara was enjoying her first spoonful of sweet potatoes when the doorbell rang.

"Oh that must be Joleen, your babysitter," Meaghan cheerily sang out to Tara. "You sit here while I go let her in."

Megan and Joleen returned to the kitchen, and Joleen began making a fuss over Tara. Fifteen-year-old Joleen lived next door and loved to come over and hang out with Tara whenever she could. Joleen was one of Tara's favourite people.

"Hi Tara, how are you? Do you remember me? Your Mom says we can hang out for awhile today, won't that be fun?" Joleen took over feeding Tara while Meaghan went back upstairs to get dressed for the evening. Meaghan felt full of hope.

She heard the front door open. *That must be Marty; he's home early,* she thought, and her excitement grew.

Marty came upstairs and announced in a low mono-tone, "I'm going to take a shower."

"Okay, I'm just about ready," Meaghan replied, cheerily.

Meaghan was brimming over with anticipation. She was going on a date with her gorgeous husband! *This is going to be the best evening in a long long time,* she thought.

"Happy Valentine's Day!" she sang out as Marty stepped out of the shower. Marty looked at her and didn't say a word. *He must be tired from working all day,* Meaghan thought. Meaghan's face was glowing. She couldn't remember the last time she'd been this happy. She slipped into her black skirt and took one final look in the mirror to make sure everything was tucked in as it should be. "I'm ready, I'll be downstairs waiting," she informed her husband with a sweet smile.

Meaghan went downstairs and informed Joleen about the evening's agenda. She showed her where the emergency phone numbers and her cell phone number were kept. Joleen finished feeding Tara set her out of the highchair and tidied up.

"I know you two will have lots of fun tonight. Tara just woke up, so she won't be ready for bed until about eight o'clock. If it's a little later that's okay, whenever she acts tired you just go ahead and put her to bed." Meaghan said.

"I'll take good care of her and we'll have lots of fun. Don't you worry about us, Mrs. Summers!" Jolene assured her. At that moment, Marty came downstairs, looking very handsome in his faded blue jeans and crisp white cotton long-sleeved shirt. His blonde hair was still damp, and the slight stubble growth on his face gave him an attractive rugged look. Meaghan let out a whistle. "You look mighty handsome, my man." Meaghan informed him.

"Thank you," Marty replied as he acknowledged her compliment with a weak smile.

Meaghan and Marty said their goodbyes to the two girls and headed out the door. Marty got behind the steering wheel of Meaghan's well-used mini van, and Meaghan climbed in beside him. "I'd like us to stop at Hattie and Harry's house if you don't mind," Meaghan said. "I need to borrow a shirt from her."

"Okay," Marty replied.

"Tell me about your day," Meaghan requested, once they were on their way.

"Oh, just another day on the construction site, exactly like all the rest," Marty said. They drove in silence until they reached Meaghan's sister's house. Meaghan opened the vehicle door and then stopped to ask, "Are you coming in?"

"I'll just wait here," Marty responded.

"Okay, I won't be gone too long," Meaghan sang.

Meaghan hurried into the house and greeted her sister with a hug. "Oh, I've missed you." she told her sister. "Hi Harry, how are you?" she asked, when she spotted her brother-in-law sitting in his favourite chair in the living room.

"I'm good, Meaghan—look at you! You are absolutely glowing! What's going on with you? Is that a new hairdo?" Harry asked.

"I don't think so Harry, just happy," Megan responded with a little chuckle.

"And where's that husband of yours? We never see the two of you anymore," Harry continued.

"Oh, you know how it is, work, work, work," Meaghan replied.

"Come on in here, Meaghan, let's see about that shirt," Hattie invited.

The sisters went into Hattie's bedroom and found the perfect shirt for Meaghan. It was a deep raspberry red cotton and featured three tiny covered buttons at the neckline and an empire waistline. The material was cut to fit loosely around Meaghan's growing tummy, flattering her figure. When she walked back into the living room, Harry let out a whistle and said, "Wow, your husband is one lucky man. Are you sure you don't have a new hairstyle?"

"Oh Harry, thanks. It must be my new hairstyle!" Meaghan giggled and winked at Hattie. "I have to run. I hope we can see more of you two soon." Harry and Hattie both agreed and Meaghan dashed out the door and into the waiting van.

"All ready?" Marty asked as he started the van.

"You bet!" Meaghan replied.

The couple drove in silence to the restaurant, each seemingly lost in their own thoughts. Meaghan was itching to tell Marty about the baby, but she wanted to bring it up at exactly the right moment. Timing was everything. She was trembling with excitement. It would be hard to wait. They arrived at the restaurant and were shown to their seats.

Their waiter came over and Meaghan noticed his name badge said Horheigh.

Meaghan settled into her chair and began to relax, letting out a long sigh. "Why are all waiters named Horheigh?" Meaghan asked Marty with a little chuckle.

"I wouldn't know." Marty replied.

"So what are you hungry for tonight?" Meaghan asked.

"I'm not sure; I'll have to have a look at the menu. I haven't been here in a long time." Marty replied.

Horheigh came to take their drink order. Meaghan ordered hot peppermint tea and also a glass of ice water with lemon. Marty ordered a beer. The couple were handed dinner menus and Horheigh left.

"This pecan-crusted fish dish sounds really good, doesn't it?" Meaghan asked as she scanned the menu. "Or maybe I should order the spaghetti. Remember I used to love their baked spaghetti?"

"Meaghan?" Marty said.

"Yes Marty, what are you hungry for?" Meaghan asked. "Isn't this a great place, it's been way too long since we've been here, but it still looks exactly the same as I remember it."

Once again Marty interrupted her chatter. "Meaghan?"

Meaghan looked at Marty and smiled at him. "Marty, thanks so much for this evening, it means so much to me."

"Meaghan, if you can stop chattering for five minutes, I have to tell you something."

"I've got something to tell you too, Marty, but you go first, I can hardly wait!" Meaghan responded.

"Meaghan, I want a divorce!" Marty replied.

Meaghan looked at Marty. "What did you say?" she asked. Hurt and bewilderment spreading across her face.

"I'm leaving you," Marty repeated.

"Right now, we haven't eaten yet!" Meaghan replied.

"Meaghan, I don't want to stay married to you. I'm moving on." Marty told her.

A country song about "moving on" danced through Megan's head. She shook her head as the realization of what Marty was saying hit her; the colour drained from her face. "I don't understand what you're saying." Meaghan responded slowly.

"I'm leaving you. Our marriage is over."

"But…I love you, and we have a daughter. How can you leave your daughter?" Meaghan wailed.

"Meaghan, you have always been a way better parent than I have. Tara is better off without me. I don't seem to have any connection to her!" Marty stated.

Meaghan was stunned. "No connection! What about blood? You have a blood connection! She's your daughter." Horheigh delivered their drinks. Meaghan stood up quickly, and turning to leave the table, almost lost her balance. Horheigh reached out and caught her arm. "Easy, lady," he said, showing concern as he steadied her.

"Thank you, Horheigh," Meaghan offered with a faint smile. "We're leaving."

Marty reached into his jeans pocket and pulled out a crumpled twenty dollar bill. He dropped it onto the table and he and Meaghan walked out of the restaurant. Horheigh quietly watched. They climbed into their vehicle and drove to their home in silence.

"You're home early, Mr. and Mrs. Summers," Joleen exclaimed when she saw them coming into the house. "Is something wrong, Mrs. Summers? You look kind of pale."

"We've had a change of plans for this evening, Joleen. How is Tara? Where is she?" Meaghan questioned the sitter.

"I've put her to bed, Mrs. Summers. After her bath we read some stories and played some games, and then she started rubbing her little eyes, so we got her jammies on and I just finished putting her down."

"Thank you, Joleen. I appreciate all that you do for us," Meaghan told her. She walked over and gave Joleen a gentle hug. "Mr. Summers will pay you and see that you get home safely—good night Joleen." Meaghan said.

Marty walked outside with Joleen and paid her, then he watched her walk home to the house next door and go inside. Marty then turned around and went back inside his house. He looked at Meaghan.

Meaghan looked back. Finally in a dull voice she said, "Lock the door on your way out."

And with that she turned and walked up the stairs to her bedroom.

Chapter 7

GROWING

Upon checking into the Sunrise Inn in the city of Saskatoon, Anna began unpacking her worn burgundy leather valise. Earlier that morning, she had driven into the city from Loon Creek. Once Anna had her belongings stowed away in her more than luxurious hotel room, she ran a steaming, fragrant bubble bath, quickly undressed and stepped into the water. Slowly she let out a long deep sigh and began praying.

"Heavenly Father, Thank You for this golden opportunity. I trust that you will help me to not make a complete fool of myself in this presentation today. Guide me to be an inspiring weight-loss ambassador and to promote the healthy lifestyle that I know You want me to live by. My Heavenly Father, I trust that Your Holy Spirit is with me on this journey, and I look to You for peace. In Jesus' name I pray, Amen."

When Anna finished praying, she tried her best to relax. She wanted to be well-rested and looking her best for the afternoon meeting. Finally she would get to meet the other four contestants. There was one from the four western provinces—British Columbia, Alberta, Saskatchewan and Manitoba—that one being Anna. There was one from Ontario and Québec, one from the Maritime Provinces, one from the Northwest Territories and one from Nunavut. Anna was sure she'd been told that there would be ten or more contestants. *They must have made some changes to the original plan,* she thought.

Anna would also be meeting with the Senior Weight Loss people from the Enlighten Company who would provide valuable information concerning how the program actually worked as well as exercise routines and the general agenda for the upcoming tour. During the next week, the contestants would learn proper makeup application, deportment, and choosing the most suitable clothing for their body type. Anna was thrilled about every aspect of the program.

Before Anna had left Loon Creek that morning, she had begged Silk to drive into the city with her. Although Silk was excited for her, he wasn't interested in going to the city. Silk and heavy traffic just weren't compatible. He didn't like that it took him a long time to get from point A to point B, and he certainly wasn't afraid to tell anyone how he felt about cities, therefore he opted to stay home.

Anna stepped out of her refreshing bath and wrapped herself in a gorgeous, soft, sea-green oversized bath towel. She twisted a smaller towel of the same colour around her wet hair and began drying herself. When she was dry, she lathered moisturizing body butter over her body and worked diligently at rubbing it in. After hanging up her wet towel, she covered herself with a beautiful, plush, strawberry-pink bath-robe unwrapped the towel from her head, and shook her hair loose.

Anna felt that her hair was beginning to thin, and the thought of that really bothered her. She'd have to ask the "hair people" what could be done for her problem. After carefully applying her makeup, she dressed herself in an elegant navy linen suit and a raspberry-coloured silk blouse. The colour brought out the pink in Anna's cheeks, giving her a radiant glow, but she felt tired.

I shouldn't be tired—I had a good rest and a wonderful bath. It must be all the excitement! Anna thought.

The phone rang. "Anna, its Sara, are you doing okay? How is your room? Don't you feel just like a queen with such a gorgeous room?" Sara asked all in one breath.

"Yes, I do Sara. So glad you called. What time are we supposed to meet everyone—and where?"

"Just go down to the lobby when you're ready. We'll meet the rest of our group there at about five o'clock. I think they're planning on serving appetizers and making introductions in the lobby, and then going into the formal dining room for dinner. The Chairperson will hand out our itinerary for the next couple of days. Are you almost ready?"

"Yes, I am. Just a couple more minutes, and I might add that I'm about as nervous as a schoolgirl on her first date."

"Don't worry, you'll do wonderfully. Just try to relax. I'm ready to go down to the lobby now, so I'll be there to meet you when you're ready."

"Okay, Sara, and thanks for all your support and encouragement," Anna replied.

"No problem, kiddo. See you downstairs." Sara said, and hung up the phone.

Once again Anna whispered a silent prayer, thanking God for this amazing opportunity. She gave herself one last primp in the mirror and let out another long sigh. She really was nervous.

Here goes, she thought. *My spiritual gift from God is encouragement, so I'll do my best to be a positive role model and encourage the other contestants.*

Pleased with how she looked, Anna reached for her little silver evening bag, hung the strap over her shoulder and headed out the door.

As promised Sara was waiting downstairs in the hotel lobby. "You look stunning, Anna," Sara gushed.

"And you as well, young lady," Anna responded. There were a few people gathered in the hotel lobby, but none of them were known by either Sara or Anna.

"I don't know if these people are from our group or not, so let's go find our banquet room; it's room number three," Sara suggested. The women joined arms and went in search of the designated banquet room. Sara and Anna entered the beautifully-decorated chamber and couldn't believe their eyes.

The room was lavishly adorned with shimmering silver pots full of blooming plants. Huge blossoms appeared in every colour imaginable, and some that Anna had never imagined. Their fragrance was breathtaking. Rainbow-coloured balloons were hung from the nine-foot-high ceiling to span across the entire ballroom, in the shape of a rainbow.

"Oh, look at that," Anna announced. "There is a pot of gold at the end of the rainbow!"

Sure enough, sitting at the end of the beautiful man-made rainbow, was a huge bronze pot filled with hundreds of gold coins. The room was made up in a fairytale setting and Anna felt like she was a princess.

Sara and Anna strolled around the room, admiring the decor. Occasionally other people entered the room and were transfixed at the setting, just as the first two ladies were.

Eventually a female voice interrupted their observations. "Ladies and gentlemen—if there are any gentlemen here," she paused and looked around. "Oh yes, I see a couple of gentlemen—welcome everyone." She smiled and continued. "It's time for our evening to begin. The servers will be passing out appetizers and drinks, so please help yourselves as they pass by. You all look fantastic, by the way, and doesn't this room look like a scene from a princess movie? Let's begin by introducing our beautiful contestants. From what I've seen, I think the judges are going to have a very tough job ahead of them choosing only one finalist to be our Ambassador for Enlighten Weight Loss. Let's start in the east, from the Maritime Provinces, which includes New Brunswick, Newfoundland, Labrador, Nova Scotia, and Prince Edward Island. Ladies and gentlemen, please welcome Elena McDonald."

An elegant middle-aged lady stepped forward and slowly walked toward the speaker, who continued. "Elena is fifty-two years old, stands five feet nine inches tall, and has lost fifty-seven pounds with the Enlighten Weight Loss Program. Let's hear a big round of applause for Elena."

Elena turned to the audience, gave everyone a big smile, bowed at the waist, and then quietly returned to her seat.

The emcee went on. "Next from central Canada, which includes the provinces of Québec and Ontario, ladies and gentlemen, I would like you to welcome Michelle Leblanc."

Michelle stood and made her way to the speaker. The emcee continued. "Michelle speaks both English and French fluently; she is twenty-eight years old and is five feet eight inches tall. Michelle has lost a total of seventy six pounds with the Enlighten Weight Loss Program. Way to go, Michelle!" The audience clapped appreciatively and Michelle returned to her seat.

"Ladies and gentlemen, our next representative is from Western Canada, which includes the provinces of Manitoba, Saskatchewan, Alberta and British Columbia. Please welcome Anna Baldman. Anna is fifty-four years old, her height is five feet one-and-a-half inches tall, and she has lost twenty-three pounds with the Enlighten Weight Loss Program. Congratulations, Anna!"

Anna stood up and walked to the front of the room. She turned to face the audience, gave them a big smile, a casual wave, and then returned to her seat.

"Now from the Territory of Nunavut, we have Galilani Agliara. Ladies and gentlemen, please welcome Galilani. This young lady is forty-three years old, is five feet and five inches tall, and has lost fifty pounds with the Enlighten Weight Loss Program."

Galilani's facial features proved her Eskimo heritage. She sauntered gracefully towards the speaker, and turned and waved at the audience. The audience seemed thrilled with Galilani and showed their appreciation with loud applause.

"Our last and final contestant is from the Northwest Territories, ladies and gentlemen. Please welcome Paj Morrison. Paj is our youngest contestant at age twenty-six. Her height is five feet four inches, and she has lost a total of forty-four pounds with the Enlighten Weight Loss Program. Paj, what an interesting name, perhaps later you will tell us what it means?"

Once again the audience showed their appreciation with loud clapping. The speaker continued. "We do not have a contestant from the territory of the Yukon. That is disappointing, but we understand there was no one available to make a year-long commitment for this tour." The announcer continued. "Thank you very much, lovely contestants. Now that we've met all of you, I would just like to make a few announcements. To the decorating committee: wonderful job, thank you. It feels like a wonderland paradise in here."

The emcee carried on with her housekeeping announcements and Anna became lost in her thoughts. She still could not believe that she was playing a major role in all this excitement. The announcer's voice broke through Anna's thoughts. "Ladies and gentlemen, I have one quick but very important announcement. One of the judges has just handed me this information. These five ladies altogether have lost a total of two hundred and thirty pounds. What a feat, great job ladies, and now we are about to be served a delicious dinner, and while this is happening, I would like you to sit back, relax, and enjoy our incredible entertainment. Our entertainer this evening will be performing on the harp. Ladies and gentlemen, please welcome Angela McCord."

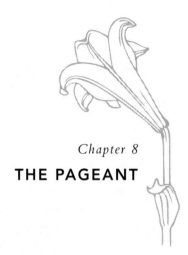

Chapter 8

THE PAGEANT

Angela played the last lingering note of her beautiful ballad. After much applause, the guests once again focused on the drama about to unfold. "Ladies and gentlemen, you've met our five glamorous contestants for the Enlighten Weight Loss Competition. I will now ask these five participants to come forward." The emcee announced.

Anna nervously rose from her chair and walked on stage along with the four other contestants. "Ladies, we are going to ask each one of you why you feel you would make the best representative for The Enlighten Weight Loss Program for Canada. After this first round of questions, the audience will place a vote as to who they think should be our Canadian representative. Your evaluation should be based on the participant's answers as well as their poise and demeanour. The two contestants with the lowest number of votes will then be eliminated. The three remaining contestants will be asked various other questions, testing them on the weight loss program as well as their knowledge of our beautiful country, Canada. The judges will then decide whether or not their answers are acceptable. If the contestant is not sure of an answer or answers incorrectly, it will obviously be detrimental to her, and the audience will be made aware of the error. Now, let us begin at the east coast of Canada, Miss Maritime, will you come forward please?"

The first vote eliminated Elena from the Maritime Provinces and Galilani from Nunavut. The three remaining contestants were Michelle, the little French mademoiselle from Québec City, the beautiful Paj from the Northwest Territories, and Anna, the vivacious middle-aged woman from western Canada.

The three ladies stood facing the audience. Anna was trying very hard not to show her nervousness when the first question was directed at her. "Tell me Anna, what is the one thing that you love most about Canada and why?"

"That is a great question!" Anna exclaimed with a little smile. "There are so many marvellous facts about Canada—one being the breathtaking physical beauty of our country. But I will choose the one that I think is the most significant. I believe that Canada is the best country to live in because it's made up of countless nationalities and cultures. It's a huge melding pot of colours, religions and beliefs, and we are all accepted for who we are. I don't think any other country in the world is as free and accepting as Canada. There were five of us here representing the Enlighten Weight Loss Group. Each one of us with a different background and heritage, and none of us will be judged by our colour or religion. We will be judged by our ability to perform the required duties. That's what's so great about Canada!"

"That is an excellent answer, Anna—thank you.

Now, Michelle from Central Canada, would you tell me about your province of Québec? Please share with us what the main industries are, and the population. Also, what political party is in office at this time?"

Michelle took a deep breath and slowly began to answer the questions. She spoke in English, but her French accent was very pronounced. Everyone listened respectfully. "I am most happy to answer these questions for you, Madame. Québec City, of course, is the capital city of Québec, and is the most populated city in this province after Montréal. At present the political party in power is the Parti Québécois. At last census, taken in 2006, the population was one million and two hundred thousand—this includes the entire metropolitan area. Ten percent of these people work in the manufacturing industry, and the other ninety percent of the jobs are concentrated in public administration, defence, services, commerce, transport and tourism. CHUQ, Central Hospital University of Québec, employs more than ten thousand people."

The judges were very impressed with Michelle's knowledge of Québec and thanked her for her answers. The emcee along with the other guests applauded long and loudly. When the applause ended, the emcee announced, "That was very informative—thank you, Miss Central Canada."

The emcee moved on to Paj—Miss Northwest Territories. "First of all, please tell us about your name. It is very unusual. Is there a story behind it?"

"The name Paj has several meanings," Paj began. She paused and looked around the audience before she continued. "It can mean pie, or beautiful, also shy, or willing, or flower. In my culture, there is no such thing as boy's names or girls names. Girls usually take on the names of their grandfathers," Paj explained.

"Thank you, Paj. Now will you tell me about your territory? I would like to know when it was established as a territory; it's my understanding that Nunavut actually broke away from the Northwest Territories. Can you tell me the details of that episode? I would also like to know your capital city, and the main industries of your home territory."

Paj took some time to ponder the questions and then replied, "Nunavut broke away from the Northwest Territories and became its own territory on April 1, 1999. Actually, that's what happened to pretty well all of the Canadian provinces throughout the years. These territories were created in June of 1870. At that time, the Northwest Territories included almost all of non-confederation Canada." Paj paused for a moment and then continued. "The capital city is Yellowknife, and the current Premier is the Honourable Bob McLeod. The government operates under a consensus system. There are no political parties in the Northwest Territories—just one Premier and six ministers."

"The major economic resource of the Northwest Territories is minerals. Mining, commercial fishing, forestry and tourism are all primary economic activities.

Reindeer are raised in northern MacKenzie." Personally I think these are for Santa Claus," She added with a smile. "Trapping has become less significant, while soapstone carving by the Inuit has become more important, however mining accounts for 25% of the annual gross domestic product."

The emcee thanked Paj. "That is most interesting," she said. The audience showed their appreciation with applause and then she continued, "We'll take a fifteen-minute break now, giving the judges time to review the answers and verify them. Please feel free to get up walk around, and help yourself to refreshments."

Sara and Meaghan rushed over to hug Anna. "You did great, Anna!" Meaghan gushed.

"Where did you come from?" Anna asked her.

"I had a hard time getting away from home, but I came as soon as I could. I heard all the questions and the whole panel discussion. It was great! There were some really thoughtful questions and answers." Meaghan responded.

"I think everyone's answers were smack on, and they both deserve to win this contest," Anna said. "I'm going to go congratulate Paj and Michelle on a job well done."

"We'll go with you," Sara said. Meaghan, Sara, and Anna linked arms and went in search of the other contestants. When they came across Paj, Anna wrapped her arms around her and exclaimed. "You are a winner, Paj. You present yourself very well and you're oozing poise!"

"Thank you, Anna. If I were voting, I'd vote for you," Paj said, returning the hug.

Just then, Michelle made her way over and joined the group.

"Congratulations, you two!" she exclaimed. "You both did amazingly well. I don't know which one of you I'd vote for, that is, if I could vote," she said with a little chuckle.

"Thanks Michelle. Your presentation was very professional," Anna told her warmly.

The contestants and guests mingled around the room, sampling the mouth-watering fruit trays and savoury delicacies that seemed to appear from nowhere. Anna walked over and poured herself a cup of hot tea, and then she, Meaghan and Sara slowly wandered back to their chairs.

Sara looked anxiously at her watch. Thirty minutes had passed with no judges in sight. *They must be having a really difficult time deciding,* she thought.

"Ladies and gentlemen take your places, please," the emcee announced. The three contestants quickly walked back to their seats on the stage. The head judge walked up to the microphone and said, "There were no errors in any of the answers, so therefore there will be no disqualifications. It is a very tight match. So we, the judges, have decided to let you, the audience, make the final decision. You will each be given a ballot with the three contestants' name on it. You will place an X by the name you wish to vote for."

The ballots were handed out and silence filled the room as each voter marked their ballot. The judge added, "Each one of these contestants has her own very unique personality and style. These three ladies are definitely all winners, and any one of them would make a perfect candidate for the Enlighten Weight Loss Ambassador. However, we have to choose one." There was a slight pause while the ballots were collected. She then continued. "The judges will take some time to count your ballots, and then you will be informed of the result."

The guests once again started chattering in anticipation. Some made their way to sample more delicacies. Michelle, Paj, and Anna formed a little group with Meaghan and Sara. "If I'm not chosen winner this evening, I just want you all to know that I'm off to France to begin a career in journalism," Michelle informed them.

"Wow, how exciting! What happens to that if you are chosen?" Sara asked.

"I guess my career in journalism would have be put on hold for a year," Michelle replied, flashing a sweet smile.

"And Paj what about you—what were you involved in before this competition?" Meaghan asked her.

"I'm actually a nanny by trade," Paj replied. "Before this competition came up, I had just received an offer to travel to Africa with a group of young doctors to care for their children while they set up a medical clinic."

"Jumping jackrabbits!" Anna exclaimed. "You two certainly lead exciting lives—France…Africa. I feel like I must be pretty boring with competition like this!"

"Oh look, here come the judges!" Meaghan informed the little group.

The head judge approached the microphone and began. "Ladies and gentlemen, we have the decision you've all been waiting for. The race was a very close one, as I'm sure you will all appreciate. But by popular opinion, and with the judges' approval, the winner of the title Miss Enlighten Weight Loss will be given to Mrs. Anna Baldman from Western Canada!"

Cheer and whistles filled the room. Everyone stood up and clapped. Anna was in a daze. *How can this be?* She thought. *I'm just a little insignificant woman from northern Saskatchewan.*

YOU ARE MY CHILD AND I LOVE YOU. YOU CAN DO ALL THINGS IN ME. Anna knew this was affirmation from God. She stood up and walked up to the platform. The judge hugged her warmly and said, "Congratulations, Anna. You deserve this title, and I know you will perform your duties with grace and charm."

Another judge stepped up to the stage and presented her with a huge bouquet of red roses. She kissed Anna on her cheek and congratulated her.

"Thank you," Anna replied. "Thank you all. You have all been very kind and encouraging. It is an honour to represent this organization. Everyone here has been a blessing to me. I will certainly try my best to live up to your expectations."

The audience encircled Anna, embracing her and bestowing all their good wishes on her. Many extended invitations, encouraging her to look them up when she passed through their corner of Canada on her tour. Tears flowed freely by contestants and guests. A warm and loving spirit could be felt in the room and left everyone very emotional. Addresses were exchanged. Anna was overwhelmed by this response and encouragement. Slowly everyone began filing out of the room.

"Anna, before you leave, let's set up a time to get together and plan your itinerary. I have a tentative schedule set up for you, but I know you're too over-whelmed to talk right now. How about we meet for dinner tomorrow and discuss the details of your trip?" The name badge pinned to the judge's suit said her name was Cerle.

"That sounds great, Cerle," Anna responded. "And you're right—I'm way too overwhelmed with emotion right now. I need to call my husband. He won't believe this!"

Chapter 9

THE ODYSSEY BEGINS

Anna couldn't believe that she'd been chosen as the weight loss representative for Enlighten. To say she was overwhelmed was a huge understatement! She shakily dialled her home phone number, and in a very unsteady voice told her husband the news. She vaguely remembered Silk whooping and hollering and congratulating her at the other end of the line. She thought she'd told him that she'd be home day after tomorrow, but the rest of the conversation was a blur!

The minute Silk hung up the phone; he got busy arranging a secret congratulatory barbeque party in his wife's honour. He jotted down a guest list which included family, several of their neighbours, and all of their closest friends. *Fifty is a good number,* he thought. Planning a party was a skill Silk knew he lacked; that duty in their marriage had always fallen on Anna's capable shoulders, so he decided to hire a local caterer to help him manage the fine details. *Anna will be home*

Friday. Sunday will be the perfect day for the party, Silk thought, getting more excited by the minute. *This will be awesome!*

Anna arrived home late Friday night, and by the time Saturday rolled around, Silk was ready. He had to tell Anna about the barbeque—he was too excited not to share it with her. Anna wasn't sure she wanted all the attention, but Silk prevailed saying, "It's all planned, you can't do anything about it. So just relax and enjoy."

The evening's festivities began at five o'clock with hors d'oeuvres and cocktails being served. Then, Silk proposed a toast to his beautiful wife. "My friends, you all know Anna and what an amazing person she is. The reason we're all gathered here today is to pay tribute to my Anna for competing and winning the title of Ambassador for the Enlighten Weight Loss Company in Canada. This great honour had been bestowed on Anna, and everyone that knows her can appreciate how hard she works to keep herself in top shape, physically, mentally and spiritually. Anna, here's to you; we are all aware that you are very deserving of this award." Silk raised his glass and toasted, "Anna, my beautiful wife, may God continue to bless you richly on your journey across Canada, as I know you will bless others that you come in contact with. Friends, please raise your glass and drink with me to Anna!"

Glasses were raised and clinked together as everyone responded to the toast.

The caterers had arrived at the house early that morning to decorate the back yard and set up tables and chairs.

Silk decided to go with a Canadian motif, since Anna's new role was Ambassador of Canada. Small circular tables hidden beneath white damask table cloths covered with tiny red maple leafs were placed strategically throughout the backyard. The napkins were made of red damask and folded to look like little Royal Canadian Mounted Police hats. These were stacked on a side table. Overhead, red and white crêpe paper streamers were woven together to look like a sunset. The tail end pieces of the crêpe paper were braided together for twelve inches and then the remainder was left free to wave in the breeze. The entire circumference of the back yard was marked off by red and white helium balloons strategically placed among the natural green shrubbery.

A live band was playing old time rock and roll music in the background and the colourful balloons appeared to be dancing and bobbing in time to the music.

The party food had been prepared elsewhere by the caterers and brought over just before the guests arrived.

Silk was wearing a dazzling white cotton polo short-sleeved shirt which accentuated his deeply-tanned face and arms. His slim-fitting permanent-pressed khaki trousers suited his strong muscular torso, and he looked trim and relaxed in his role as master of ceremonies and husband of the guest of honour.

Once again, Silk stood up and clanked his glass for attention. "My dear friends and family," he began, "I want to humbly thank you all for coming to our little gathering this evening. Your presence definitely makes this celebration very sweet. As you can see, I am extremely proud of my beautiful wife. She has reached a personal goal in her life and is able to step out of her comfort zone and take on this Canada-wide trip in order to promote the Enlighten Weight Loss Program. Because of this, I want to toast all of you—our guests. Victory in life would be shallow without family and friends to share it with us, friends, here's to all of you!"

Again there was much clinking and laughing as the guests raised their glasses and acknowledged the toast. Silk continued. "I would like to share a little story with you about an experience Anna had this past week.

As I'm sure you all know, Anna leaves for Saskatoon tomorrow to begin the first leg of her journey. Being the good little wife that Anna is, she insisted on preparing an abundance of meals and leaving the deep freezer full of them for me. At the same time, she was trying to clean the house, plus tackle all the packing and planning she has to do to be ready for her tour. I kept telling her it's not necessary, but of course she won't listen to me!

Well, yesterday morning, Anna drove down to Johnson's store to pick up a few groceries. At the checkout, she took her wallet out of her purse and paid for her purchases with her credit card. She left the grocery store, taking a quick look back to make sure nothing was left behind on the checkout counter. Then away she went, pushing her shopping cart containing three shopping bags and her purse. She loaded the shopping bags and her purse into the back of her van, pushed the grocery cart over to a raised cement pad, parked it, then walked over to her van, climbed into it and drove away.

"On her way home, Anna noticed an old unkept woman with grey matted hair hobbling along the sidewalk, pushing a doll's stroller. The tiny stroller was loaded down with what Anna thought must be the woman's earthly possessions. Anna remembered seeing this person earlier in the day, feeling sorry for her and thinking, *she must be living on the street*. Anna passed by the woman and continued merrily on her way home.

"She got about half-way home when she spied a large cardboard sign on a heritage house boldly advertising 'RUMMAGE SALE INSIDE.' Anna felt compelled to stop—she hasn't yet learned how to pass by a second-time-around sale. After parking her van, she hopped out and went in to have a look around. Deciding there was nothing she needed; she walked back to her van and continued on her way home.

Nearing the Excell Pharmacy, she remembered there were a few items she wanted to buy for her trip and decided to stop and pick them up. She grabbed her purse off the van seat and headed inside the store.

"As she stepped inside the store with, her purse slung over her shoulder, she became aware that her purse felt very light. I'm sure most of you know that Anna is paranoid about losing her wallet so she quickly opened her bag to make sure that it was tucked safely inside. It wasn't there!

Hurrying quickly back to the van, her first thought was that she must have thrown it into one of the grocery bags at Johnson's store. She rummaged through her three cotton grocery bags but it wasn't there, either. Anna climbed into the van, behind the steering wheel, planning to drive back to the grocery store. She looked through her purse once again, no wallet. She opened the van door, stepped out and walked around to the back. She checked through the grocery bags once again; emptying each bag until she got to the bottom. There was still no wallet so she climbed into the van and drove back to the grocery store. Anna was in full panic mode by this time, but she started praying, 'God, please let someone find my wallet and turn it in to the cashier.' Anna knew that a lot of people lived on the streets by the grocery store, and if she had dropped it outside she may never see her wallet again. Her panic increased!

"As she neared the grocery store, Anna heard a calm reassuring voice tell her, 'IT'S OKAY, WE'LL FIND YOUR WALLET, DON'T PANIC.' *Don't panic?* She thought. *My wallet has my life in it. My identification, my credit cards, my driver's license. Don't panic!* Anna wanted to panic; she felt like she deserved to panic. The voice said again, IT'S OKAY, WE'LL FIND YOUR WALLET, DON'T PANIC. *Okay,* Anna thought. *God is telling me, 'don't panic!' so I won't.*

"Anna calmed down and experienced peace, that she knew had to come from God. She completed her drive back to the grocery store parking lot and parked her van near to where she had left her shopping cart. She couldn't believe that her grocery cart was still in exactly the same spot as she'd left it; and there was something dark lying on the bottom of the cart. She ran over, and there was her wallet with the picture she carries of the two of us staring up at the sky. Checking through the contents, Anna realized that everything was there. She just couldn't believe it and she thought. 'God, You are so AMAZING!'

"Anna was overjoyed! She raised her arms into the air and shouted. 'Thank you Lord!'

After the discovery, Anna climbed back into her vehicle and started home. She found herself humming a tune as she drove along, completely carried away by God's goodness.

Once again, she passed the homeless lady with the doll stroller limping along. Anna told me that she remembers thinking '*Poor thing. What a sad lifestyle living on the street.*'

When Anna arrived home, she quickly called our daughter, Cindy, on the telephone; she was so excited and jubilant about finding her wallet that she wanted to share the news. She just couldn't stop praising God.

Anna told me that her hand was shaking when she dialled Cindy's number and Cindy told me that even her mom's voice was shaking when she answered the phone.

Anna told our daughter what had just happened with her wallet and how amazing and wonderful God is. She went on to tell her that there was one thing that bothered her though and that was that she didn't think she had honoured God through it all!

Cindy asked her mother what she meant.

Anna told her that as she had been driving home after finding her wallet intact, and had seen what appeared to be a homeless woman wandering along the highway pushing a little doll stroller filled with what looked like her life's possessions in it, and Anna had just driven right by her! God had just blessed her immensely, and here was this poor little old lady walking along the street with basically nothing, and she had driven right by.

Once Anna got home and realized fully what happened she felt that she should have stopped to see if there was anything she could do to help her. Maybe she should have given her some money.'

Cindy was impressed with her mother's candidness and asked her "'do you think you should have?'

Anna told her that she really believed that God was putting it on her heart to stop and give her something, and she hadn't listened. She told Cindy that she was going to drive back to the grocery store and try to find the street lady. She felt that if someone had found her wallet and taken it, she would have been left with nothing, but He had blessed her and now she needed to pass on the blessing.'

Cindy expressed that she felt her mom was pretty awesome for feeling that way and told her so.

"Anna went to her purse took out a twenty dollar bill and stuffed it into her pocket. She grabbed her car keys and headed out the door."

Silk was struck with emotion as he told the story about his wife. He wiped tears from his eyes. "God is truly a God worth honouring and obeying. Friends, let's make a toast to our God and His abundant goodness."

One of the guests shouted out, "Tell us the rest of the story, Silk! What happened to the old lady?"

Silk continued. "Well, Anna drove back to Johnson's Grocery store, searching for the woman so that she could pass on her blessing, and she did pray that she would find her. Upon arriving at Johnson's store she scanned the area.but there was no homeless woman to be seen, so Anna turned the car around and slowly drove back home. She never did see the woman again." Silk continued. "I spoke to Anna about this later, and she was feeling very badly about missing the opportunity to bless the old lady, but says she did learn a valuable lesson from this experience. That is, she will try to be more aware of the suffering of those around her. We shouldn't have to go through some trial ourselves to be more open to the need of others." Silk raised his glass and took a sip of his drink. "Hopefully we can all follow that advice."

Chapter 10

MEAGHAN

With Marty gone, Meaghan and Tara adjusted to living alone, and their lives fell into a familiar routine. Due to the fact that Marty hadn't really spent much time at home, it wasn't terribly difficult for either of them to get along without him. Tara hardly ever mentioned her dad.

Beautiful, baby Cohen was born in September close to his due date. When Meaghan's delivery time drew near, her parents insisted that Tara and Meaghan move in with them. They didn't like the idea of the two of them living alone in case Meaghan should go into labour. On September 5 at nine o'clock in the evening, in her parent's home, Meaghan wearily climbed into bed beside Tara.

Meaghan had felt energized all day. She and Tara had taken a long walk to the park and played on the swings and slide, and now they were both exhausted. Tara fell asleep instantly, and Meaghan let out a contented sigh as her head sank into the soft white down pillow. No sooner had her head hit the pillow when she immediately sprang up again! *Oh no!* She thought, *I guess this baby has other ideas for me tonight.*

Meaghan felt a surge of warm, sticky liquid running down between her legs and knew that her water sac had erupted. She swung her legs over the side of the bed and slowly climbed out, being very careful not to disturb her sweet little Tara. Reaching for the clothes she had just taken off, she slowly redressed herself and walked out of the bedroom and into the living room where her parents were watching the evening news on television. "Whats happening honey, you look a little pale." Her mother asked as she anxiously rose and touched Meaghan's forehead.

"My water just broke, Mom—in your bed!" Meaghan wailed.

"Oh Meaghan," her mother exclaimed, gathering her daughter into her arms. "Oh honey, how marvellous, our precious little one is almost here. Dad will drive you to the hospital. I'll stay here with Tara. You go – go!"

Meaghan picked up her small previously packed overnight case handed the bag to her dad, and they were off to the hospital.

Cohen's birth progressed fairly easily and quickly. As Meaghan waited for her doctor to arrive she felt the baby slide down into the birth canal, and Meaghan told the nurse that it "was time". The nursing attendants tried to tell Meaghan that it would be quite some time before this baby would arrive, but they were wrong. Meaghan's labour intensified rapidly and she felt the urge to push.

Suddenly, from out of nowhere the doctor appeared, and Meaghan was wheeled into the delivery room. A few minutes later, with a mighty yelp, a tiny little red baby his head covered in thick black hair appeared, and Cohen made his grand entrance into the world.

"It's a boy." The doctor said. At the same time the nurse exclaimed, "It's a girl!"

Meaghan shook her head in confusion looking from one to the other and asked, "What is it?"

The nurse gently swaddled the child in a lovely soft blue flannel blanket and placed him into Meaghan's waiting arms. "He's a beautiful boy," the doctor and nurse both concurred.

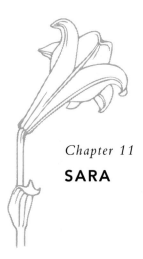

Chapter 11

SARA

Sara heard her phone ringing and hurried to answer it.

"Hi Mom, it's your favourite son, Luc."

"Luc, hi - where are you?" Sara asked.

"I'm at home, Mom, in Calgary. How are you doing?" he asked.

"I'm fine, honey. What's going on with you? You hardly ever phone when it's not Sunday or my birthday!" Sara replied with a little laugh.

"I'm okay, Mom. I just wanted you to know though that Lisa and I are history. I finally caught up with her and she's decided to go ahead with the abortion. I've been praying and praying that she wouldn't, but she's got her mind made up and I can't change it."

"I'm so sorry, honey. Can I do anything to help?"

"I don't think there's anything anyone can do, except I know you like to pray," Luc answered.

"I will, Luc, and you don't give up on praying either," Sara answered solemnly. "When can you come out and visit me? You know how much I miss you."

"I don't know, Mom, I'm kinda down in the dumps right now. Maybe a visit to see you would be a nice change."

"Why don't you take a few days off work and come to Saskatchewan. It won't change the facts about the baby, but it might take your mind off of it for awhile." Sara asked.

"Okay Mom, I'll try and figure something out at work and let you know the plan. Oh, and Mom, thanks for not being judgemental or condemning. I am just as responsible for this problem as Lisa is, right?"

"I know you are Luc, but that's something you'll have to work out with God. It's not my job to blame anyone."

"Well, thanks for that, Mom, I appreciate it. Your support is important to me, you know that, right?"

"Luc, I'm sure you're aware by now that I'm one of your biggest fans. You could never to anything to make me stop loving you—or giving you my unsolicited opinion."

"I am beginning to realize that, Mom, thanks. I'll call soon. I love you too—oh, and Mom?" Luc said.

"Yes?" Sara asked.

"I'm not going to give up begging Lisa not to have an abortion until she either listens to me or she goes ahead and does it!" Luc stated.

"I think that's a wonderful idea!" Sara replied.

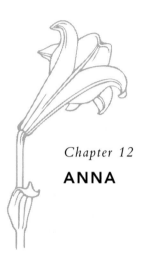

Chapter 12

ANNA

Anna stuck her hand into the mailbox, picked out some letters and flyers and carried it all into her house. Leafing through it as she made her way, she noticed a big fat brown envelope from the Enlighten Weight Loss Company. *Oh, it's here my schedule, she thought.* Dropping the mail on the kitchen table, she slit open the brown envelope and began to read. Enlighten requested her presence in Saskatoon on Wednesday of that week for her first official assignment. She was to meet the Chief Executive Officer from the Weight Loss Company at the Travelcity Hotel. The letter told her where to sign the official documents, making her legally the Ambassador of the Enlighten Weight Loss Company. The plan was for her to stay in Saskatoon for a week and familiarize herself with her upcoming position; she would get her official itinerary for the year, plus participate in the required training.

Wow! This is really happening. I still can't believe it, Anna thought. *I'd better go through my clothes and make a list of what I need to take and what I'll need to buy. Looks like I start my tour in Vancouver. I wonder what the weather is like in Vancouver in May— what kind of clothes should I take along?*

Anna found herself humming softly as she proceeded to go through her closet, sorting her clothes. An hour later she heard the front door open. She called out, "Is that you, Silk? I'm in the bedroom."

Silk walked into the bedroom, reached out to give his wife a hug and said, "There you are. I've been missing you all day. What are you so busy doing?"

"I got my official package today!" Anna exclaimed. "I start my tour on Wednesday in Saskatoon. They want me to stay there for a week to get everything in order, and there's some training involved; then it's off to Vancouver to start the tour."

"Good for you, Anna. You've worked hard for this. I hope they treat you like a queen! But you know, I'm going to miss you terribly. What am I going to do without you?" Silk grumbled.

"You could come with me, Silk." Anna suggested.

"I'll come with you to Saskatoon, how's that? We can spend as much time together as they'll allow us in between your training sessions."

"Oh, that'll be great, Silk. That will get me off on an excellent start."

Anna continued sorting through her clothes. Silk left her to it and went into the living room to watch the midday news on television.

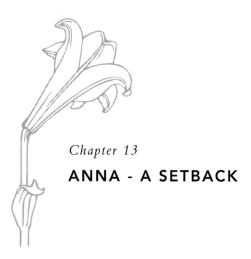

Chapter 13

ANNA - A SETBACK

On Wednesday, Anna and Silk left home early, anticipating the three-hour drive to Saskatoon as requested, to begin the Enlighten Weight Loss Program journey. The Enlighten director had a luxurious hotel suite reserved for them at the Travelcity Hotel located on the west end of the city. To Anna's relief, Silk offered to do the driving. Anna couldn't believe how tired she'd been feeling lately. It must *be all the excitement and extra work I've been doing to get ready to go on this tour,* Anna thought.

Silk stopped the van in front of the Travelcity Hotel, and said, "You go ahead and check in, honey, while I find a parking spot. I'll bring in the luggage."

Anna flashed Silk a grateful smile and asked, "How am I going to manage without you on this tour? Are you sure you won't come with me?"

"You'll be totally lost without me, but you will manage," Silk assured his wife with a smile.

Anna proceeded into the hotel lobby, dug into her purse for her credit card, and presented it to the clerk at the front desk. The reservation was confirmed, and Anna was given a room number along with two door passes. As she was signing the hotel contract, the concierge brought over a plainly-wrapped, sealed package and handed it to Anna saying, "This came for you, Mrs. Baldman."

Anna took the package fumbled in her jacket pocket for some change for a tip and handed it to the attendant. Silk walked into the hotel laden with luggage. "Are we all checked in?" he asked.

Anna nodded her head up and down.

"Great, let's go find our room," he said. "Lead the way, sweetie."

Anna led the way to the elevator with Silk following close behind her, pushing a trolley laden with the luggage. She pressed the appropriate floor button, and they stepped into the elevator. Upon arriving at their appointed room number, Anna unlocked the door and held it open for Silk as he juggled the bags into their room. Once everything was inside, Anna quickly slit open the brown paper package and began to read the letter inside.

"It looks like we're to meet with the Enlighten Chief Executive Officer for dinner at six o'clock tonight at the Rib Place on Sixth Street!" Anna informed Silk. She went on to say, "Silk, have I told you how excited I am to be here? I have to keep pinching myself to make sure I'm not dreaming."

"I think you told me one hundred and twenty five times…or was it only one hundred and twenty four?

But come on over here and let *me* pinch you for awhile. Have I told you how many times I'm going to be missing you while you're off touring the country?"

"I think you only told me one hundred and fifteen times—you have some catching up to do, Silk Baldman! You know I do feel bad about leaving you. But not bad enough to stay home!" Anna replied with a giggle as she reached up and slipped her arms around Silk's neck.

"Not bad enough to stay home with me, you say woman?" What if I tell you that as the head of this house you MUST stay home and look after your husband, whether you like it or not?" Silk teased as he reached out and started tickling Anna. The tickling led to touching and cuddling. "We have lots of time before dinner. What say we make good use of it?" Silk asked his wife in a voice husky with emotion.

Anna and Silk undressed quickly and made their way into the bedroom. Once under the covers, Silk nuzzled Anna's neck and murmured, "I love you, Miss Enlighten," and continued to demonstrate his love to his beautiful wife.

Some time later, Anna slid quietly out from under the covers and tiptoed into the bathroom. She ran a steaming hot bath and poured a cup full of sweet-smelling calming bath salts into the water. Climbing into the tub, she settled in for a nice long soak.

Twenty minutes later, emerging from the bathroom and wearing a long soft, fuzzy pink bathrobe, Anna checked on Silk and noticed that he hadn't moved an inch since she left him sleeping on the king-sized bed. Anna changed into a new chocolate-brown two-piece skirt suit under which she wore a teal blue silk camisole.

Around her neck she carefully wrapped a scarf in a colorful mixture of deep brown and teal. She then slipped her tiny, freshly-manicured feet into suede, chocolate brown sling-back pumps. Her dark blonde newly styled hair was cut in a becoming short, layered bob. "Wow, you look and smell good enough to eat," Silk commented as he rolled over and caught a glimpse of his beautiful wife.

"It's almost time to go—you'd better get up and get dressed, sleepy head!" Anna teased Silk. "Besides, you've already had your dessert. I still can't believe this is happening! This wonderful golden opportunity has come at the exactly the perfect time in my life. Have you ever noticed how God's timing is always perfect? I think I'm all ready to go."

"That's my girl!" Silk said as he quickly dressed himself. "Now I'm starving for some real food. Let's go find some dinner."

Anna and Silk walked out the door arm in arm into the elevator and zoomed down to the main floor. "Let's take a taxi to dinner. Then I don't have to worry about fighting the traffic and finding a parking spot once we get there," Silk suggested.

"That's fine with me," Anna responded happily.

Anna and Silk were met at "The Rib Place" by the Committee members from the Enlighten Weight Loss Company. The prearranged dinner was beautifully prepared and served, and the Enlighten entourage treated Anna like a celebrity. She was presented with her itinerary for the first month of the tour. The couple thoroughly enjoyed their evening; they were wined and dined in style. When the meal and presentation were over, Silk hailed a taxi and they headed back to their hotel.

Upon arriving at their room, Silk said, "Anna, there's something I need to show you, come here a minute. I noticed it earlier when we were making love."

"What is it, Silk?" Anna asked in a strained voice.

"Come!" Silk said. He reached over and slipped off Anna's jacket. He lifted her camisole, unclasped her bra and gently touched a spot on her left breast. "You have a lump here." He told his wife sadly.

"I do? Why didn't you tell me?" Anna asked, her voice rising.

"I wanted you to enjoy this evening. There's time enough to talk about it now."

"Oh, Silk. What should we do? Should I cancel my trip?"

"Why would you want to do that, Anna? We don't have any idea what this is. Let's just get it checked out and then we'll decide what to do. It's probably nothing," Silk replied.

Anna rubbed her fingers over the lump. There was no mistaking it. There was a mass about the size of a walnut, only flatter.

"Let's pray about this before we go to bed, Anna. We both know that God is in control of everything. Let's ask Him to give us peace and courage. One of the Bible verses I've memorized is in the book of Matthew chapter six verse twenty seven: 'Who of you by worrying can add a single hour to his life?' Let's try to leave this problem in God's hands. They are most capable," Silk said.

After the prayer, Silk and Anna got ready for bed. Anna wanted to leave the problem in God's proficient hands, so she tried very hard not to think about it.

Silk was feeling rotten about having to tell Anna. He felt responsible, like he had somehow betrayed her. These feelings were gnawing away at his insides, but he tried not to think about it. He didn't want to take it back from God. They climbed into bed, curled up in each other's arms, and tried to fall asleep.

The next morning, Anna woke up refreshed and praising God. She stretched out in a long leisurely stretch.

"Thank you, my Heavenly Father, for providing me with a restful sleep. You have indeed given me comfort and peace, and I feel wonderful," she prayed. She touched her breast. The lump was still there. She swung her legs over the side of the bed and began her morning exercise routine.

Some time later, Anna searched in the phone book for the name of the walk-in medical clinic she had noticed the day before. She remembered seeing one on Saskatchewan Drive on their way into the city. When the number was located she called it and persuaded the receptionist to book her an appointment for ten o'clock that morning. At nine forty five, Silk drove Anna to the clinic.

"Silk, there's a little coffee shop over there on the corner—why don't you just wait there for me?" Anna suggested. "I can do this, I'm sure everything will be fine. You know there's no history of breast cancer in my family." Anna stretched up on her tippy toes and planted a kiss on Silk's lips. "I'll see you soon," she said.

"Are you sure you don't want me to come with you?" he asked. Anna waved him away and said, "No, I'm fine. You go and grab a cup of coffee."

Inside the doctor's examination room, Anna showed her lump to the doctor. He examined the mass with his fingers.

"Umm…there is definitely something here," he murmured. "How long have you had this?"

"We just discovered it yesterday," Anna replied.

"Well, we need to perform a biopsy to see what we're dealing with. Can you go to the lab at the City Hospital right now?" the doctor asked. "I'll make the arrangements."

"Oh, of course, I can go right away," Anna replied.

The doctor wrote out the required requisition for Anna and cautioned her with some advice. "You know, it's hard not to worry, but try not to. We don't know anything at this point."

Giving the doctor a thin smile, Anna left his office. Silk was standing outside the van drinking black coffee from a white Styrofoam cup.

"How'd you make out?" he asked.

"We need to go to the City Hospital and have a test done," Anna replied.

"That was quick," Silk said.

Thirty minutes later, Anna changed into the standard stylish powder-blue hospital dressing gown wearing the opening facing front. She watched the lab attendant prepare a syringe to perform the required biopsy.

"Now, where did you say that lump is?" she asked Anna.

"It's here." Anna pointed to a spot on her left breast with her right hand.

The lab attendant inserted the syringe into Anna's breast and extracted a bit of thick, yellowish matter. "I don't think that's quite enough—I'm going to try again." The attendant announced. She prepared another syringe and repeated the procedure. A bit more of the same substance was extracted. "That should be enough; I'll check this out right away. Would you mind just waiting here to make sure we have enough sample? I'll let you know when you're free to go."

"Yes of course—and thanks." Anna replied. She picked up a magazine and mindlessly leafed through it.

A few minutes later, the attendant came back and told Anna that the sample was enough to test, and that her doctor should have the results by noon. "I appreciate your prompt attention—thanks again." Anna said.

"No problem—you just happened to pick a quiet time around here, which doesn't happen very often," The attendant replied.

At eleven-thirty, Anna received a call on her cell phone from the doctor's office asking her to return to his office. They arrived as requested, and he beckoned them inside. The look on the doctor's his face gave nothing away as Anna and Silk walked inside. When they were both seated, the doctor said, "Anna, you're certainly entitled to get a second opinion, but it seems that from the sample we extracted there is definitely some malignant cells; and in my opinion, we should get that lump out of your breast as soon as possible. I don't know if the cancer cells are all contained in a sac or if they've already spread to the surrounding breast tissue, so the quicker we get this matter taken care of the better." The doctor informed her.

"Whoa, you started shooting with both barrels!" Silk exclaimed.

"But how is that possible? I don't understand. We just found the lump yesterday. How could it have spread already?" Anna asked.

"Cancer works in mysterious ways, Mrs. Baldman. I wish we knew more about it. Sometimes by the time we find it, it's already spread farther than you would think possible. However, that being said, there are many types of cancers, and some are very slow-moving— perhaps we'll get lucky and discover the one you have is a slow mover."

Anna took a minute to digest the news. Silk reached over and held her hands. Neither of them spoke. Finally, Anna said, "We need some time to think about this. Can we call you?"

"Of course, here's my card. I'll be in the office today until five o'clock and back again tomorrow at eight a.m." The doctor replied.

"If we do decide to go with surgery, how long is the waiting time? Will you take off my whole breast, or just the lump—and what about after surgery? Will there be any treatments?" Anna asked in a bewildered voice.

"At this moment, I can't tell you exactly how long the waiting period would be without checking with my receptionist, but it's usually about two weeks, hardly ever longer than that—and yes, there most probably will be some form of chemotherapy or radiation treatments following the surgery. I don't know how much if any of your breast will have to be removed, but once we get inside we'll be able to tell. If the cancer has spread to the surrounding breast tissue, then I'm sorry to say we may have to take your whole breast." The doctor replied solemnly.

"Okay, well, that gives us something to think about doctor, thanks so much for your kindness and your prompt attention to this. Now I need to get some air," Anna said, and stood up to leave.

Silk rushed ahead and opened the office door for her. He took Anna's arm and steadied her as they walked to the parking lot. The blood had drained from Anna's face, leaving her as white as a ghost. Neither one said a word. Silk assisted his wife into the van then reached over, grabbed the seat belt and buckled her in. He gently closed the door. "I need to cancel my trip with Enlighten." Anna let out in a hoarse whisper.

Silk looked in Anna's direction. "Are you sure that's what you want?" he asked, and then continued. "Oh Anna, I'm so sorry."

"I have to; it's not fair to them to have a sick contestant. They need someone who's healthy and vibrant and strong. I wouldn't be focused on the job anymore," Anna said. She paused a moment, then continued, "About what the doctor said—do you think we should get the test redone at another clinic and get a second opinion? It is possible there could be a mistake."

"Well, honey, I don't know if that's possible. I'll phone the doctor and ask him what the chances are of that when we get back to our hotel room. You know I'm behind you one hundred percent, whatever you decide. It just doesn't seem fair that you should have to give this up. You deserve this more than anyone, and I know and you would have done an excellent job."

"Thank you Silk, for your constant support and encouragement. I was looking forward to this trip a lot, but apparently God has other plans for us. You talk to the doctor, and then we'll decide what to do next."

Silk drove back to the hotel, and once there, he called the doctor's office and spoke to Dr. Michaels. The doctor assured Silk that any chance of test error was extremely unlikely, but they were certainly entitled to get Anna retested if that was their wish. After their talk Silk felt reassured that the tests had been preformed to the highest possible standards. The down side of that, was the fact that Anna had cancer.

The couple spent the better part of the afternoon discussing the diagnosis and their options. Finally, Anna picked up the phone and dialed the number she had been given for the Enlighten Weight Loss Company.

"Could I speak to Laura please?" Anna asked.

Laura couldn't believe the news that Anna relayed to her.

"Anna is this for real? Are you sure? Don't you want to get a second opinion?" she asked.

"What I really want is for this conversation to not be happening. I want this lump in my breast to go away. I want to forget this day ever happened and I want to go back to being happy and healthy and carefree." Anna paused and then continued. "Do I want to get another opinion? My husband and I are confident that the test results are accurate. We don't believe it will change a thing! I guess what I want right now is for you to let me out of this contract without any hard feelings. I need you to find someone else to send on the tour. Selfishly, I plan on taking care of my health and I don't want to feel guilty about letting you down." Anna was babbling, and tears were streaming down her face. Silk was watching. He walked over to Anna and took the phone from her. "This is Silk, Anna's husband," he said "Anna needs to go now. I'm sure you'll need time to digest this news—please get back to us when you can." Silk hung up the phone.

Wrapping his arms around his wife, he led her to the arm chair. Sitting down, he pulled Anna onto his lap, where she curled up in his arms and cried like a baby while he rocked her gently. Finally his wife stopped crying and relaxed. She let out a big sigh. Silk continued rocking and humming softly until his beautiful wife fell asleep in the security of her husband's strong arms.

Chapter 14

REGROUPING

Sara's legs gave out beneath her and she sat down on a kitchen chair with a heavy plop. Silk had just phoned to tell her about Anna's diagnosis.

"Anna has breast cancer, no way!" Sara just couldn't believe it. Wasn't *that every woman's worst nightmare?* Sara wondered. She was absolutely stunned.

"Poor Anna, I can't imagine what she must be going through! What, I wonder, *what* can I do to help?" she asked herself out loud. She continued pondering the situation and remembered Enlighten. *Enlighten—what will Enlighten do? Anna can't possibly be thinking of going on the tour now. I never asked Silk if they've told Enlighten yet. I'd better call Meaghan and fill her in. Maybe she can help me wrap my head around this,* Sara thought.

Sara went to the phone searched for Meaghan's phone number, and with fumbling fingers found it and dialed. When Meaghan answered she said. "Hello Meaghan, is that you? It's Sara calling."

"Yes, Sara, it's Meaghan. How are you?" Meaghan asked, delighted to hear from her friend.

Sara decided to get right to the point. "I'm fine, but you'd better sit down; I have some very disturbing news."

"Oh Sara, what happened?" Meaghan asked apprehensively.

"It's Anna, Meaghan." Sara replied, and then went on to say, "Anna has breast cancer!"

"No way, Sara, I know you wouldn't kid me about something like this, but it's hard to believe—she looks so great and healthy! How long since she found out? Where is she? What can I do?" Meaghan asked, her words coming out in a rush.

"I don't know what to do, Meaghan, except pray for her and Silk. They're in Saskatoon right now, and I understood Silk to say they only found out themselves a couple of days ago. I believe she's been placed on a waiting list for surgery. They're hoping the surgery will take place in about two weeks." Sara replied.

"What about Enlighten and Anna's tour?" Meaghan asked.

"That's exactly what I was thinking. I forgot to ask Silk if he's informed Enlighten, but I'm sure he would have. I'll call him back and ask him. I just wanted to share this with you first." Sara replied.

"Thanks for that Sara, let me know what you find out," Meaghan said, and hung up the phone.

Sara dialed Anna's cell number. Silk answered.

"Silk, it's Sara. I'm sorry to bother you, but have you informed the Enlighten group about this?" Sara asked.

"Yes, Sara, we have told them, and they were very gracious and let Anna out of the contract," Silk told her.

"Oh good, that's one less thing you have to worry about," Sara said in a relieved tone.

"You know Sara; we are making every effort to not worry about this. It's certainly thrown a kink into our plans, and I'm not trying to make light of this situation, but women battle and survive breast cancer every day. Anna and I are striving to leave this in God's hands and keep a positive attitude," Silk replied.

"Good for you, I admire your attitude, Silk. I know that God will bless you for it. Please remember that Meaghan and I will be praying for Anna, and you," Sara said.

"Thanks Sara, we appreciate that very much," Silk said, and with a thoughtful expression clicked off his phone.

Sara's phone rang the second she hung up with Silk.

"Hello," she responded.

"Sara, this is Laura, I'm the current Chief Executive Officer with the Enlighten Weight Loss Program," A voice stated on the other end of the line.

"Oh yes, hi Laura, what can I do for you? Sara asked.

"Sara, have you heard about Anna Baldman's diagnosis?" Laura asked.

"Actually, Laura, I just found out this morning. Do you know what's happening with the tour? Are any of the other contestants able to step in and take over?" Sara inquired.

"That's what I'm calling about, Sara. I've spoken to each of the other four ladies that made it to the finals, and they've all taken on other commitments for this year, so I'm thinking it might be difficult to find someone who's available for this tour. What do you think?" Laura asked.

"Well, I'm not sure. What are the options?" Sara asked.

"Sara, our company truly appreciates the fact that it was you and Meaghan who were responsible for finding Anna, and she was an excellent candidate. You know many of the members in the Enlighten organization, and we were wondering if you two could possibly find another contestant that would meet the requirements. Of course, they won't have to go through the whole elimination process again; there's just not enough time for that. Is there any chance you and Meaghan would be willing to do this for us?" Laura asked her.

"Laura, I'm flattered that you think we could do this, thank you. I'll talk to Meaghan and we'll let you know. But just so you're aware, right now, there's not one person coming to mind that would be suitable for this position!" Sara replied.

"Sara, I know you two will do your best. I'm going to leave this with you, and I trust you will let me know if you can come up with any names," Laura assured her, and clicked off the connection with Sara.

Sara put the phone back on its stand and sat for a few minutes thinking about the assignment. *I need a cup of hot tea,* she thought. *Hot tea always helps me think.*

Taking her favourite strawberry china tea cup out of the cupboard, she plugged in the kettle and made herself a cup of steaming, fragrant peppermint green tea. Then she sat back down, picked up the phone, and once again dialled Meaghan's number.

"Meaghan? It's Sara again," she said when the phone was answered.

"Sara, hi, what's happening now?" Meaghan replied.

Sara filled Meaghan in on the proposal from Laura regarding the Enlighten Weight Loss's search for another contestant.

"Gee, that might be a tough assignment," Meaghan said, expressing concern.

"I know, Meaghan. Can you think of anyone at all that has the requirements and the time to go on this tour?"

"I'm trying to think of all the gorgeous women we saw at the last convention; of course we don't know if any of them would be able to give up their careers or other full-time commitments for a year," Meaghan wondered, out loud.

Suddenly it seemed like a light went on in Sara's head. "I know!" she practically shouted into the phone. She was so excited she could barely talk; she started stammering, "*You*, Meaghan, *you!* You would be perfect for the job. You have every qualification we're looking for!" Sara's voice was rising, becoming shriller as she continued on her train of thought. "I don't know why I didn't think of it sooner. You're so right for the job! I can't imagine anyone who would be more perfect! You're gorgeous, you don't have a job! You love travel-ing, you—"

"Whoa, not so fast, girl friend," Meaghan inter-rupted Sara in an amused voice. "It may seem to you and perhaps many other people that I don't have a job because I stay at home and work, but I do have a very important job, *two* very important jobs—actually three. My first two jobs are the most significant ones in the whole wide world and that's taking care of my two adorable little children every minute of every day. The three of us are a team, and we want to stay that way, thank you very much. My third job is as an online sales marketer for a small Canadian company. I put in forty hours every week, doing online marketing for this company. It pays the bills."

"Oh Meaghan, I'm so sorry, of course I know that you've chosen to be a stay-at-home mom, and I admire you for that; I did completely forget about your online marketing position. Please forgive me." Sara stated seriously. "But I really do think you should consider this other position."

"Of course I forgive you, Sara; the marketing position I could give up and possibly get back a year from now, but I certainly can't give up my children for a year. That's ridiculous!" Meaghan responded.

"I could look after them for you, Meaghan," Sara responded in a quiet voice. "How old did you say they are? I know," she said getting more excited by the minute. "If the company approves, the children and I could go on tour with you. You would be with them every day!" Sara's voice became louder and bolder.

"Tara is five and Cohen is almost three," Meaghan answered. "Sara, they are so sweet, they're my life, and I couldn't imagine leaving them for even one day, let alone a whole year." Meaghan shared some of her children's latest antics with Sara. Her voice became soft and husky with emotion when she spoke of them. Sara listened intently to Meaghan's stories about her children. The children sounded adorable. Sara loved being a gramma. She often thought that if someone had told her how much fun grand mothering was, she would have opted to be a grandmother instead of a mother. Then with a little chuckle she came back to the present. Looking after Cohen and Tara and touring across Canada with them and Meaghan sounded very appealing to Sara. "Your children sound adorable, Meaghan. Would you consider taking me on as their nanny if the Enlighten Company approves of me and your children traveling with you?"

"Sara, are you sure? You haven't really thought this through. You know that I appreciate your offer tremendously, I can't think of anyone I would rather have as a caregiver for my children, but this is so sudden. It's one thing to baby sit your grandchildren for a couple of hours a day, and another thing entirely to have two little people underfoot every day for a whole year!"

"Meaghan, we will share in the care of your children. You know that when you have free time I will gladly hand them over to you and I'll take a break, but when you're busy working I will be their caregiver, and I'm sure I'll love every minute of it. Will you at least think about this, Meaghan? Can I call Laura from Enlighten and ask her if the company will consider this option?"

"Well, I guess it won't hurt to ask them. I'm not against the idea, it's just so sudden. See what they have to say about it, and remember this would be a huge commitment for you as well as for me; you have to be sure it's what you want!" Meaghan informed her friend.

Sara went on, "Meaghan, before we go any further, let's just take a few minutes and pray about this. God knows our every desire, and He has a plan for each one of us. We need to make sure we're being obedient to His will."

"Oh course, Sara, that's a great idea. Let's pray together and see what God has in mind for this situation, then we'll leave it in His hands," Meaghan replied.

The women prayed to God over the phone, and then said their goodbyes.

Meaghan hung up the phone and sat down, holding her head in her hands. What an overwhelming day so far—first hearing about Anna's sickness, and then the offer from Sara to go on a year-long tour with her as the children's caregiver. *It's almost unbelievable*, Meaghan thought. She lifted her head and let out a little chuckle. *I think my life is becoming a soap opera.* Meaghan prayed again. *Is this offer from you Lord? You know how lonely I get sometimes. Is this trip your answer to that loneliness?*

Suddenly, Meaghan felt a sense of peace come upon her. She got the impression that God was telling her, "YES, IT'S OKAY, I WILL BE WITH YOU ALWAYS." God would be with her and her children, and He would never leave her nor forsake her. She also sensed that because Sara was a God-loving woman, she would be a good influence for Tara and Cohen, and nurture them with godly love, kindness, and discipline.

Meaghan felt at peace. "Thank you, my Lord," she stated.

At Sara's house, she put down the phone. Sara couldn't believe the offer she'd just made Meaghan. *Where did that come from? What am I doing? I'm almost sixty years old. I have a grown-up family. Do I have enough energy to run after these two little people every day for a whole year?* She asked herself. "Oh, but it would be so much fun, God!" she answered herself out loud. "Maybe it will bring some life back into this old girl." She continued thinking, *I have so much love to give away, and I believe those two little children and our beautiful Meaghan need some lovin' badly. It would give me a purpose again!*

Sara knew that since her dear husband Bill had passed away, her life had drifted along without any particular direction, and now she felt ready to get behind the steering wheel of her life again, as a co-pilot to God, and with His help, to form a new life that would have some purpose. "My Father in heaven, please hear my prayer," she prayed. "You know what's on my heart. I feel that I have a lot to offer these two little children and their dear mother. Please guide me in the direction You want me to go. I want to do what's acceptable to You. In Your precious Son Jesus' name I pray. Amen."

Sara too felt calm and at peace after her prayer. She went to the sink, rinsed out her tea cup, and then went outside to pull some weeds in her vegetable garden.

Sara hauled out tools and stakes and was busy staking her tomatoes when she heard a cheery, "Hello?"

Chapter 15

LUC

Sara stood up and brushed the garden debris off her jeans. Turning around, she let out a happy shriek as she spied her son, Luc.

"Well hello back at you, my boy!" Sara exclaimed excitedly. "What are you doing here?"

"I came to see my favorite mother. Is that alright?" Luc asked, teasing her.

"Exactly how many mothers do you have?" Sara teased back, and then added. "How long can you stay? Can you stay for the whole weekend?"

"Yes, I can stay for the whole weekend, Mom. I have a couple of days off so I came to relax and hang out with you." Luc said.

"I'm so glad Luc. What can I get you? Would you like a cold drink? A hot drink or something to eat?" Sara was so excited to see her son that she became flustered.

"I'm fine Mom. I can grab myself a cold drink when we go inside. What are you doing out here? Do you need some help?" Luc asked his mother.

"Well, actually I could use a little help, you came along at just the right time. I'm having a hard time pounding these stakes into the ground. Would you do that for me? I need one beside each tomato plant." Sara replied.

"Glad to help." Luc said. He grabbed the hammer and started pounding a stake into the ground beside each plant. Sara wrapped some twine around the heavy plants and secured them to the stakes. When the task was complete, Luc wiped imaginary sweat from his brow with the back of his hand. "Now I'm ready for that cold drink, Mom. Let's go inside, it's hot out here."

Luc and Sara went inside and Luc grabbed two cold sodas from the refrigerator. "Do you want one of these, Mom?" he asked her.

"Sure that's fine, a cold drink on a hot day is perfect," Sara said. As they were sipping their drinks, Sara brought up the subject of Lisa. "I'm anxious to know if you've heard anything from Lisa." Sara asked her son.

"Mom, I've been trying to call Lisa almost every day for about a month. All I get is a recorded message saying, 'I am not available for your call right now, please leave a message and I will return your call as soon as possible.' Luc replied, trying to change his voice to sound like a girl. I've tried calling her cell phone and she won't answer. I even phoned her parents to see if they could or would give me a valid number. They must be away because they haven't returned my calls either. I don't know what else to do."

"I'm sorry Luc—surely she must have call display, and know that you've been trying to reach her. Can we pray together about this?"

"Mom, I know you think prayer is the answer to everything, but I'm just not there. I don't have much of a relationship with God right now, but if you want to pray, you go for it, I would just rather not. I'll keep trying to find her at least until I know the baby is safe. I've driven to her apartment a few times and sat outside in my car watching for her. I haven't so much as caught a glimpse of her, I hope no one is watching me—they'll think I'm a stalker."

The conversation came to a lull as both Sara and Luc reflected on the situation.

Suddenly Sara burst out, "Luc, I do have something to tell you. If my plan works out, it's going to change my life, for a year anyway. Do you want to hear about it?"

"What kind of question is that—do I want to hear about it, when it's life changing?" Luc asked in a bantering mood a big grin spreading across his face.

Sara continued. "Luc, have you ever met my friend Meaghan from my Enlighten Weight Loss Group?"

"No Mom, I don't think I've ever met any of your friends from that group. Why?"

"Well, it's a long story, so sit back and I'll tell you all about it!" Sara informed her son. She took a deep breath and proceeded to tell Luc about Anna, and how she was chosen to be the Enlighten Weight Loss representative for Canada, and then about her diagnosis of breast cancer. At that point Luc cut in and said, "Oh, Mom, I'm sorry, that's very sad. What is her prognosis?"

"It's too early to know, honey. I just found out today, and she's only known for a couple of days. I think she's set for surgery in about two weeks. Anyway, she can't go on the Canada-wide tour, so the company asked my friend Meaghan and I if we would try and find someone to take her place."

"Don't tell me—you're going to take up the reins and become Miss Canada for your weight loss group?" Luc asked excitedly.

Sara burst out laughing and said, "Oh Luc, thank you for thinking so highly of your old mother, but no, I'm not at all qualified for that position."

"Not qualified? You're in the best shape ever, and the best darn looking sixty-year-old woman I've ever laid my eyes on!" Luc objected.

"I think you might be just a little bit prejudiced, thank you, but no, it's not me, but it might be my friend Meaghan. Luc, she's absolutely gorgeous, and if the Enlighten group approves of my idea, she will be Canada's representative"

"So what does this have to do with you, Mom?" Luc asked.

Sara continued to tell Luc about her plan to be nanny for Meaghan's children on the tour. When she finished, Luc let out a long, low whistle and exclaimed, "Wow, that's a pretty heavy commitment, Mom. Are you sure you're up for that? How old did you say these kids are?"

"The oldest one is a little girl named Tara, and she's five. The little boy, Cohen, is almost three. I haven't met them yet, but according to Megan, who I'm sure is not exaggerating one little bit, they're adorable. Did I tell you Meaghan is a single mom? Her marriage broke down before Cohen was even born; I know this is a huge undertaking Luc, but I really feel it's time I started living again. I've been mourning your dad for a year and a half, and this might just be my opportunity to get out and start a new life. It will certainly give me a valid purpose for the next year, plus I'll see some of Canada!" Sara ended her spiel with a note of excitement in her voice.

"You're amazing, Mom! If you feel this is right for you, and if you're up to the challenge, then go for it. It sounds like you're really excited about it, so good for you! It will be great to hear little feet running around the house, and I've always wanted a little brother and sister!" Luc said with a chuckle as he walked over and hugged his mom.

Chapter 16

MEAGHAN - MOVING FORWARD

Meaghan went outside to look for her children; it was bath time. Out of the corner of her eye, she thought she caught a glimpse of something pink hurrying behind the garden shed. She decided to play along. "Tara, Cohen, time to come in for your bath." Meaghan called.

No answer.

I bet they're playing hide and seek. I'll pretend I can't see them, Meaghan thought.

"Tara, Cohen," she called again. She announced loudly, "I guess that Princess Tara and Spaceship Captain Cohen must have jumped into their supersonic space-ship and taken a ride to the moon. Maybe if I call really loudly they'll hear me and come down from outer space."

Meaghan walked over to the swing set and called again, really loudly this time, "Spaceship Captain Cohen and Princess Tara, you have an alien looking for you. Come down, come down wherever you are! This alien has a peace offering of chocolate chip cookies and milk for you."

Suddenly, out from behind the metal garden shed, two little figures ran at full speed toward their mother.

"Mom, how did you know we were in outer space?" Tara asked.

"I want cookies," demanded Cohen.

"Whoa, not so fast, you two outer-space galactic people, this alien needs big squisher hugs before I release any confidential information." Meaghan scooched down on her haunches and stretched out her arms to hug both children at once. They came at her with such force that Meaghan lost her balance and tumbled over backwards onto the soft grass with Tara and Cohen landing on top of her.

"That was a good hug. How did I know you two flew off into outer space? This alien has six eyes and four ears. She hears and sees everything that goes on at this space centre," Meaghan said, getting into a sitting position, pulling Tara onto one knee and Cohen onto the other.

"Mom, two ears and two eyes!" Cohen stated, touching her ears and then her eyes.

"My extra ears and eyes are top secret, Captain Cohen. They might be hidden under my hair or on my body someplace where you can't see them," Meaghan informed him solemnly, rubbing her hair and her shoulders, and then her tummy.

"Mom, you do not have six eyes and four ears, you're teasing us," Tara responded, giving her mom a poke in the tummy.

Meaghan began tickling Tara, and she fell to the ground giggling. Cohen tried to tickle his mother, but her arms were longer than his and she reached over and tickled him instead. He giggled and fell to the ground too. This led to all three of them rolling around on the grass, with lots of giggling and more tickling until everyone was out of breath. This was the life Meaghan loved; she stretched out on the grass and let out a contented sigh.

Once the children regained some energy, they started running around the backyard. Meaghan raced after them, caught them, and tickled them some more. They fell to the ground once again and rolled over and over, giggling all the while. Finally, Meaghan gasped out, "That's enough; this alien needs a rest and you two spaceship people need to come in for your bath. How about we leave the cookies for after supper? What should we make for supper tonight? I bet you'd like tomato soup and grilled cheese sandwiches!"

"I want cookies!" Cohen responded.

"I know you do, but how about we have some soup and sandwiches first?" Meaghan coaxed.

"I love grilled cheese!" Tara announced, smacking her lips together.

Meaghan smiled to herself. "Have I told you two galactic creatures that being your mother is the best job I could ever have and that I love you both forever and ever and ever?" she said, stretching out her arms as if to wrap them around the whole world. She knew there was definitely no way she could live without these two children, certainly not for a whole year.

Chapter 17

MEAGHAN'S CHOICE

Sara rushed into her kitchen as she heard the phone ringing, fearing that the message machine was about to click in and she would get loud screaming in her ear.

"Hello?" she responded, quickly grabbing up the receiver and holding it to her ear.

"Hey Sara, how are you doing?" Meaghan asked.

"Oh, you know me, Meaghan; I'm always good— some days are better than others but mostly good. What's up with you, Meaghan?" Sara answered.

"I'm glad to hear you're doing well Sara. You know, I've had time to think over your proposal of going on the Enlighten tour and having you come along as the children's nanny. Sara, if that offer still stands, I would like to say thank you very much, and I accept."

"Meaghan, that's wonderful news, I'm so glad—yes, of course my offer still stands. But you know, I haven't confirmed anything yet with the Enlighten Company, because I was waiting to hear from you, but now that

I have, I'll give them a call right away and find out if they'll approve of all of us going on tour," Sara replied.

"Sara, you know that the only way I can accept this offer is if my children can come along, it's absolutely not an option for me to go without them," Meaghan said. "Their dad has been completely absent from their lives since before Cohen was born, and it would be far too devastating for them if I were to leave them as well."

"I'm sorry to hear that about their, dad, Meaghan. I don't understand how a person can walk out on their children, and not even visit them," Sara replied.

"Marty did come to see me once at the hospital when Cohen was born. He told me that he and his latest love had split up. One of his buddies had driven him there because he'd lost his driver's license for driving while under the influence—and can you believe this—he asked me to come back to him!"

"What did you say?" Sara asked.

"I told him that I would think about it and let him know at Christmastime. Cohen was born in September. You know that he never came to see us at Christmas—maybe he was scared that I would actually take him back. Anyway, that's the last time I saw him."

"How awful for you, Meaghan, you have been through a lot, but were you actually considering taking him back?" Sara asked incredulously.

"Life can be lonely on your own with two little children. I didn't make time for friends, and I guess I felt that if no one knew how unhappy I really was I wouldn't have to deal with it. So, for a couple of years I just buried myself in food. When Marty asked me to come back, he promised that he would get help for his drinking problem. I seriously considered giving him another chance, but he never came back. How gullible am I?" Meaghan sighed, and then said with a little laugh, "Anyway, the children and I are doing just fine on our own now, but I couldn't possibly leave them. I hope you understand that."

"Of course I do, Meaghan, and I've certainly entertained loneliness many times myself since my husband Bill passed away. I'm going to call Enlighten right now and tell them our plan. They'll have to take all four of us, or none. You'll be Miss Enlighten, and I'll be the children's nanny or gramma or caregiver, or whatever you want to call me. I'll let you know what their answer is as soon as I know. I'm so excited, I can hardly wait."

"Oh Sara, I'm thrilled. I think that if they approve this, we are going to have a very fabulous, exciting adventure. The trip will truly be an answer to prayer, but are you sure it won't disrupt your lifestyle?"

"Lifestyle, swifestyle," Sara mumbled. "I don't have a lifestyle or anything that even comes close to one, Meaghan. I believe that God has opened this door for me and given me the green light to go ahead." Then she continued. "Yes, Meaghan, it will disrupt my whole life entirely, but I'm so ready for a disruption. I'm going to call Laura, the Chief Executive Officer at Enlighten right now, and find out what she thinks—remember, they're having a hard time filling this position, so they might be absolutely thrilled to take on all four of us." She went on to say, "It would mean living out of hotel rooms for a year, but most hotels in Canada are pretty luxurious, with heated swimming pools and often grassy parks nearby. It's perfect, really, because your children aren't in school yet—and next year Tara will be in kindergarten, right?"

"Yes, you're right, Sara. The timing is perfect for my family. Let me know what you find out—now that I've made my decision, I'm so ready to get the ball rolling!" Meaghan said.

"I will, Meaghan. You start packing your bags. I think we're on our way to Vancouver—and the beginning of a brand new adventure!"

Chapter 18

MEETING THE LITTLE PEOPLE

Meaghan's door bell rang and she hurried to answer it, drying her hands on a kitchen towel as she went. "Come in," Meaghan sang out as she opened the door.

Sara was standing outside. "Sara, this is a surprise! What are you doing here?" Meaghan asked excitedly.

"Hi Meaghan, thought I'd better come over and meet your two adorable children since I'm going to be their nanny for the next year!"

"Are you serious?" Meaghan asked, throwing her arms around Sara's neck, she let out a happy cheer.

"Would I kid you about this?" Sara queried, grinning from one ear to the other as she returned Meaghan's hug. Stepping back, Meaghan threw her hands in the air and let out a big "WHOO HOO! Come in, quick, come in, and tell me all the details!" Meaghan insisted, leading Sara into the living room. "What made Enlighten agree to the nanny proposal?"

"Actually, they loved the idea; they think its good public relations to have your children along. Enlighten believes that the average woman will really be able to relate to a young single mother, whom I might add is gorgeous and smart, as well as being a wonderful mother role model. Our flights are booked to fly to Vancouver one week from today. Will that give you enough time to tie up loose ends and get ready to go?"

"We have to leave that soon?" Meaghan questioned. "Come," she added, taking Sara's hand and leading her into the kitchen. There they sat down at the kitchen table and Meaghan poured them each a cup of freshly brewed, hot, fragrant cinnamon tea. "Tell me—were they desperate for a contestant, Sara?" Meaghan asked once the tea was poured.

"Actually, no, Meaghan—they did come up with someone on their own. He's a man, and I think his name is Harley, or Hugo, or something like that, and he lives in Manitoba. Since they don't have that many men in the weight loss program, and practically none that are available for the trip, they were getting excited about sending a man. But, because they'd asked us to come up with a contestant, and they hadn't yet asked Harley/Hugo, they decided that you would get first dibs. So, if you're still sure this is what you want, and I'm still sure it's what I want; then I guess we're good to go!"

"Yes, I do want to go," Meaghan stated emphatically. "How about you, Sara, are you sure you want to be living out of a suitcase for the next year? You'd be giving up a lot. What does your family have to say about it?"

"I had a peek at the traveling schedule, Meaghan. It's really not that intense. There are several three and four day weekends planned throughout the months of August and September. I will easily have time to fly out to visit my children, or they might take the opportunity to come and visit me when I have a few days off. I think this will work out just fine for all of us, Meaghan. I'm really willing to give it my best shot. You know that since my Bill died, there's been emptiness in my life, and I've been searching for a worthwhile, satisfying purpose. I love children; this is going to be GRRRREAT!" Sara informed her young friend. "Now where are your children? I'm so ready to meet them!" Sara asked, standing up and looking around.

"They're playing in the family room. Come, I'll introduce you. They can be little monkeys sometimes. Maybe you'll change your mind about going with us after you meet them!"

"Not a chance!" Sara announced.

Meaghan led Sara into the family room. Tara was dressed up in a gorgeous poppy pink princess gown which consisted of layers of sparkling pink netting. These layers formed a skirt that swirled around Tara's tiny feet as she walked. A pair of clear plastic slippers which looked like glass covered her tiny princess feet. Placed atop her long white-blonde curls, she wore a shiny plastic tiara covered in jewels. As Sara and Meaghan entered the room, it appeared that the princess was in the process of changing her brother into a frog. Cohen was protesting, "I don't wanna be a frog, Tara. Turn me into a dine-sore. I wanna be a t-rex."

"There are no dinosaurs in this game, Cohen. You have to be a frog, just like in the book Mom read to us last night!" Tara exclaimed, in full control.

"Okay you two, quiet down for a minute and come here. I want you to meet my friend, Sara."

Tara and Cohen obediently came to their mother with long, sad faces. Sara took note of their sadness, but was happy to see that the children were obedient to their mother. That was a good sign. Sara hunched down on her knees to become eye level with the children.

"Hello Sara!" they both said at the same time.

"Well, hello Princess Tara and Prince Cohen," Sara responded.

"He's really not a prince—he's a frog," Tara informed Sara.

"Well he's certainly handsome enough to be a prince," Sara replied, smiling at Tara.

"I'd rather be a dine-sore, but Tara says I can't, 'cuz there's no dine-sores in the story," Cohen informed Sara.

"Well, maybe sometime we can play a different game together that has dine-sores in it. Would you like to do that?" Sara asked.

"Cohen always wants to play dinosaur games. It's not fair that we always have to play what he wants," Tara said.

"What kind of games do you like to play, Tara?" Sara asked.

"I mostly like dress-up games," Tara said, moving a little closer to Sara.

"I like dress up, but I don't wanna be a frog," Cohen wailed.

"I'm very happy to meet both of you," Sara said, reaching out and shaking their hands. "I'd like to play a game with you before I leave, but right now I'm going to go back into the kitchen with your mother and finish my cup of tea. Can you both put on your thinking caps and come up with one game that you both really like to play together?" Sara asked them.

"We don't have thinking caps!" Tara informed Sara in a serious tone. "But we like to play card games; do you know how to play card games?"

"I know some card games—why don't you two decide which game it will be? I'll be back soon, and we'll all three play a game together, okay?"

As Meaghan and Sara turned to walk back to the kitchen they heard the children begin to argue about which game they would play. "That's enough you two, no more arguing. Clean up your toys, please, and Sara will be with you soon and help you decide which game to play. I'll turn on the television and you can watch one cartoon while Sara and I drink our cup of tea. Please try and get along quietly for half an hour," Meaghan requested.

"Super heroes?" Cohen shouted.

"You always want to watch super heroes!" Tara cried out.

"I'll turn on SUPERHERO David and GIANT Goliath. How will that be?" Meaghan asked them.

"Goodie!" Cohen and Tara were both happy with that choice and settled down on the floor to watch the movie.

"Quick—let's go finish our tea while all is calm!" Meaghan suggested, tiptoeing out of the family room.

"That sounds good to me!" Sara replied.

Once back in the kitchen, Meaghan refilled their cups with hot tea. "You know, they're really pretty good kids, but this time of day can be a challenge because they're getting tired. Often I take them outside for a bit of fresh air before supper. It gets us over the hump, and then after supper they're usually ready to play together peacefully until bed time," Meaghan said.

"I'll keep that in mind, Meaghan, and don't worry. All children have their little squabbles. I'll learn their likes and dislikes. I must remember to never try to turn Cohen into a frog though, he does not like that!" Sara said with a laugh.

Meaghan replied, "Well, now you know they're no little saints. They are very much into playing pretty princesses, thorny dragons and indestructible super-heroes. Their imaginations are vivid, and they're not afraid to express their opinions."

"Good for them, those are excellent qualities. You know, when I was a child, most children were raised to be seen and not heard; I'm glad those days are over. Children are wonderful gifts from God, designed to be creative and loving; it's good to see that they're not afraid of expressing themselves," Sara added.

"So what are you really thinking, Sara? Do you think we can handle this tour? Are we women enough to pack up our bags and head off into this great big country of ours and not look back? I guess I need your assurance that we can do this together; I'm counting on you to be my support and counsel as well as my children's nanny. I know that puts a lot of responsibility on your shoulders—am I asking too much, Sara?" Meaghan asked gravely, searching Sara's face.

"Meaghan, my part of this deal is looking after your children to the best of my ability when you're not able to. I will also love to be there to give you any support, should the need arise. I'm prepared for both of these roles, and hopefully have some fun along the way. Your part of this deal is to be an ambassador for the Enlighten Weight Loss Program. You will be required to present your gorgeous self to the general public and maintain a flawless image every day, and I don't want you to be worried about your children. I'm sure there'll be challenges for both of us, but I'm so ready for a new challenge. Are you ready, Meaghan Marshall?"

"Yes, I am ready, Sara. With God's help, and with your help, I am willing to tackle this challenge! Goodbye loneliness, hello adventure. Let's call Enlighten right now and confirm with them that we're prepared to accept their agenda, and ready to get started on our new adventure!" Sara raised her tea cup in a toast to which Meaghan responded by raising her cup and clinking it against Sara's. After the clink, and with smiles lighting up both of their faces, they took a sip of tea.

Chapter 19

ANNA'S ILLNESS/SARA'S LOSS

Sunday afternoon, Sara found herself feeling a bit lonely and decided to drive to the University Hospital to visit Anna. Silk had phoned earlier in the week informing her that his wife had been called in for her surgery. Thoughts of Anna and her diagnosis of breast cancer continued crowding into Sara's mind. She hadn't been to the hospital since Bill had died, and she dreaded the thought of returning there, but she really needed to see Anna.

Upon entering the hospital, Sara searched the overhead direction board for the Oncology floor. Sara became flustered, her mind traveling in a dozen different directions, bringing back lots of painful memories of when her husband had gone through his cancer treatments and eventually his death. Sara couldn't find what she was looking for.

In the back of her mind, she felt like she was betraying Anna for finding a new candidate to take on the role of the Enlighten Representative—and Sara also felt guilty that she was getting to go on the tour as well.

Finally, spying an information desk, she proceeded to ask for directions. The kindly gray-haired man behind the desk was very helpful, and Sara expressed her gratitude.

Following the winding hallway to the elevator, Sara punched in the up arrow. She was working very hard to not allow her emotions to take control. Not only did she feel bad for replacing Anna on the tour—she felt guilty about being healthy and active while Anna was dealing with a very serious illness.

Sara entered Anna's room slowly and with trepidation. Glancing towards the bed, she saw a somewhat shrunken version of Anna. Sara gasped. Anna eyes were closed. There was a man sitting beside the bed, which Sara assumed must be Silk. Looking up from the patient, his eyes rested on Sara.

"Hello, I'm Sara," She managed to squeak out.

Silk stood up, walked around the bed, and stretched out his hand to shake Sara's. "Well, hello, Sara. I'm Silk, Anna's husband,"

Sara extended her hand in response, and they shook hands. "How is she doing?" Sara whispered, nodding her head towards Anna.

"Anna is doing very well, Sara," Silk replied with a slight smile. He pulled another chair over to the bedside and motioned for Sara to sit.

"Will we be disturbing her if we talk here?" Sara asked.

"No, I don't think so. They've got her on some pretty heavy pain medication, so we'll be alright," Silk assured her. He continued. "The doctor tells me that the surgery was successful. They did have to remove Anna's entire breast, but they're sure they've gotten all the cancer, and that after her recovery, Anna should be as good as new, minus one breast, of course.

"Of course," Sara replied. "And how does Anna feel about that?"

"You know, Sara, I've been praying about that, and I think she'll be okay with it. We haven't talked about it since her surgery, but she did mention beforehand that if this did happen, she would get plastic surgery and a new breast implant."

"You both sound very brave. I don't know if I could handle this as well as you are," Sara quietly informed Silk.

"Well Sara, I'm no great philosopher, but I think that sometimes in life we really don't have a lot of choices. Obstacles are placed in our way, and we just have to deal with them as best we can," Silk replied with a smile. "Now, tell me about yourself, Sara." Silk asked. "Anna told me that she met you through her weight loss group. Have you two known each other long?"

"No, not long at all. We actually just met a few months ago. My friend Meaghan and I were chosen to find a suitable representative for the Miss Enlighten Competition. We both agreed that Anna was the best choice, and then you know the rest. I've met up with Anna a handful of times during her training and the competition, and that's about it."

"I see," Silk said. "Well, thank you for choosing Anna to be Miss Enlighten. I don't know if you realize how good that was for Anna. It made her feel very special and unique, which I think is a first for her. Growing up

in a family of four girls, I don't think she ever thought
of herself that way.

"But what about now, with her cancer, does she still
feel special?" Sara asked wryly.

"We all know that sickness or death or divorce or
whatever can happen to anyone—and it does. No one
is immune. We all have to go through certain trials. I
believe the important thing is that we learn to become
stronger because of our trials, whatever they may be,"
Silk replied.

"My husband, Bill, died eighteen months ago," Sara
told Silk.

"I'm sorry." he responded.

"Yes, so am I. I miss him so much." Sara's eyes filled
with tears and she reached into her bag for a tissue.
"When he was dying, I wanted to die too. It's totally
devastating to lose your soul-mate. I think the only
thing worse than that would be losing a child."

"How did your husband die?" Silk asked quietly.

"He had cancer in his pancreas. There was nothing
they could do for him," Sara answered sadly. "I tried to
save him! I bargained with God for his life! I promised that I would be a better person. I'd go to church
more. I'd give more money to the poor, be a better wife
and parent. Sara paused, thoughtfully and then continued, but Bill died! I was so mad at him for leaving me.
How could he? We were a team!" Sara paused again,
deep in thought, and then proceeded. "It took me a
long time to get over being angry, next came denial,
and then depression. Depression became my best friend
and constant companion. It took me to self-pity parties
and I would cry all night long. I was overwhelmed and

in deep emotional shock for many months. I could barely function!

Now I thank God that my children and grandchildren came to my rescue and forced me to snap out of it." Tears were streaming down Sara's face and she gulped with emotion as she talked. "I'm trying very hard to learn how to live without him, but it still feels like I'm coming out of a deep fog. Often I forget that he's gone and I want to run and tell him something."

Sara began to calm down and continued. "I have three grown children, two of which are married and have children of their own. I'm a gramma three times, and it's wonderful." Sara's voice took on a more cheerful tone and she continued. "I can't imagine what my life would be like if I hadn't had a loving, supportive family to help me through this whole ordeal. And God of course—after I got over blaming God, I realized that He was my lifeline and I needed Him desperately to get through each day. He is definitely the source of my comfort and the personal peace I have that surpasses all of my understanding."

"That's amazing Sara. I admire your faith," Silk responded. "I think that faith grows on a person as you need it. God is always there when no one else is. He is never condemning, or judging, or sarcastic. He's just a thought away, waiting patiently to come into our presence to love us like no one else can."

Silence filled the room for few moments, and then Sara asked Silk, "Are you doing okay, really? Will you be alright?"

"I honestly don't know what I will do if Anna doesn't recover from this," he answered as he motioned to his sleeping wife.

Sara looked at Silk and told him, "Don't even think about that, Silk. Deal with what you know and leave the rest to God. He will get you through, either way." Then Sara abruptly changed the subject with, "Do you have children, Silk?" She asked dabbing at her eyes. "Tell me about your family."

"Anna and I have only one grown daughter, Cindy. She's married to a great guy named Hal, and they have three children. Sophie is six, Levi is four, and little David just turned two. And you're right, Sara. Family is everything, especially at a time like this," he said, pointing towards Anna's bed. "It would be pretty hard to get through something like this without my family's support."

"I need to tell you that I've been feeling guilty, Silk, about finding another contestant to represent the Enlighten Group, and abandoning Anna. You know I'm going along on the Canada tour with the new ambassador, which makes me feel even guiltier."

"Oh Sara, don't be silly. It's not your fault that Anna's become ill. I know she feels honored to have been chosen for the Enlighten position, but all that's happened since is not yours or anybody else's fault. It just happened, and life must go on," Silk admonished Sara with a stern voice.

Anna's eyes opened slowly, and she searched the room looking for the sound of the voices. Upon spying Sara and Silk, a tiny smile appeared on her lips.

"Hello Sara, how long have you been here?" she asked in a weak voice.

"Not too long, really, I'm not sure. What time is it?" she asked, looking at Silk.

"It's almost three o'clock. You've been here about an hour," he answered Sara. Then he continued with, "How are you, Anna? Are you feeling okay? Do you have any pain?"

"No, no pain. I'm fine, happy to see Sara. Silk, would you get me a drink of water please? Then I want Sara to tell me all about what's been happening with the Enlighten Weight Loss Competition."

Chapter 20

THE ODYSSEY CONTINUES

The line-up at the Coffeerama coffee shop at the International Airport in Saskatoon seemed to go on forever, and Sara stood in line waiting patiently for her turn to order. She looked lovely in her navy blue a-line skirt, and short dark denim jacket featuring three-quarter length sleeves. The soft rose hues in her silk blouse, brought out a delightful school-girl blush in Sara's cheeks. Sara's hair had been restyled for the trip, in a younger-looking, more fashionable cut. Sara had given the stylist permission to experiment with different highlight tones and she was very pleased with the end result.

I think everyone at the airport must be in line for coffee this morning, Sara thought. Airport arrival time for Sara was six a.m. The flight she and Meaghan and the children were scheduled to leave on for Vancouver was seven thirty. *And I have only myself to think about,* she thought. *I wonder how Meaghan will make out with two little people underfoot. I guess it's something a person gets accustomed to, and airports will be part of our lives for the next year.*

Just then, Sara spied Meaghan headed in her direction with Tara and Cohen in tow. Sara's breath caught in her throat when she spied beautiful Meaghan. Her long, flowing, shiny black hair hung loosely down her back and her face shone with a healthy, vibrant glow. Sara noticed that other passengers, particularly men, turned to stare at Meaghan as she made her way towards Sara. A short, taupe mini-skirt was covering Meaghan's narrow hips. Sara's eyes traveled down Meaghan's long, shapely, sun-kissed legs, and she noticed that her perfectly-shaped toe nails were painted with peach polish perfectly matching her peach tank top. Dazzling multi-coloured flip flops flopped up and down on her feet as she walked. Over the tank top, Meaghan wore a mocha-coloured cardigan with bell-shaped sleeves in a light delicate knit. A thin silver chain hung around Meaghan's neck, and her ears were adorned with silver hoop earrings. *I bet she looks beautiful in a grubby old terry towel bath robe, with curlers in her hair, and a green mud mask on her face,* Sara thought happily.

Beside Meaghan, little Cohen was sauntering along, dragging a kid-sized super-hero back pack behind him. Sara noticed his cute chubby little legs sticking out under his khaki shorts. The beautiful princess, Tara, was gracefully gliding along beside her mother, pushing a pink-wheeled princess backpack. She looked adorable, with long pink satin ribbons tying up her platinum blonde hair. The ribbons and hair seemed to bounce along in harmony as she walked.

"Over here, Meaghan," Sara waved and shouted.

Meaghan caught a glimpse of her friend and came forward with a big grin. "There you are! Isn't this something else? Where did all these people come from? Is this normal? I'm so out of the loop about airports, I had no idea it would be this busy,"

"I think everyone in Saskatoon must be flying somewhere this morning!" Sara answered, and then continued. "Why don't the three of you find a place to sit, I'll order us something to eat and drink, and then I'll join you. Tara, Cohen, what would you like to have a cranberry scone, or a blueberry muffin, and what about drinks? What would you like? Meaghan, can I get you a coffee?"

"A warm cranberry scone sounds perfect for me, Sara, and a small black coffee please. Tara, you like blueberry muffins, would you like that with some chocolate milk?" Meaghan asked her daughter.

Tara licked her lips in anticipation and replied, "Ummm, sure Mom, yes please."

"What about you, Cohen? What would you like?" Meaghan asked him.

"I wanna choclit chip muffin and hot choclit, pwease," Cohen stated emphatically.

"Is that alright with you, Mom?" Sara asked Meaghan.

"Sure, sounds perfect. Are you going to need help carrying all this?" Meaghan asked.

"I'll get a tray. You find us a table quick before they're all taken." Sara replied.

Meaghan and the children found a table covered with dirty dishes. The children sat down while Megan cleared the table. Pulling a couple of wet wipes from her travel bag, she wiped down the table, and then told her children to sit tight while she went to collect peanut butter, jelly and straws from the concession stand.

"You two don't move, I'll be right back, and I'm watching you," she admonished them as she walked the few steps to pick up the necessary items.

While Sara was waiting to order their breakfast, she started to notice the people around her. A teenage girl in front of her had three holes pierced into the side of her nose which appeared to be crusted over with dried pus. *Oh my, that doesn't look healthy!* Sara thought. Next, Sara noticed a boy teenager standing in line with an older gray-haired lady. *That couple must be grandson and grandmother,* Sara thought. The young man's long skinny blue jeans hung very low on his hips and were held in place by a woven red belt. A very long black t-shirt emblazoned with white paintings of skulls and cross-bones was tucked into his long narrow pants. *Looks like risky business to me! I wonder how they stay up when he sits down.* Sara thought with amusement.

The next couple that caught Sara's eye was a very heavy-set man standing beside a woman of the same size, getting ready to place their order at the counter. Their skin was a beautiful deep chocolate brown, and both of them were dressed completely in black. The huge man was trying to remove his very small black muscle shirt by pulling it up over his head. The t-shirt, however, was not cooperating, and the salesgirl behind the counter was trying very hard to politely tell them that they were holding up the line.

Next in the line up was a crisply-sunburned woman and man and they were definitely losing their patience. The man let out a growl, "Tell the lady what ya want already!" Mr. Sunburn, completely shirtless, was showing off a very red hairy chest and a bulging belly beneath a wide-open blue denim vest. The vest matched his partner's faded blue tattoos which appeared to cover her entire body. Mrs. Sunburn wore an ultra-short denim mini skirt which tried in vain to cover her chubby legs. Sara's eyes traveled over the tattoos covering the woman's poor scorched legs and feet wearing hot pink flip flops. Even her tiny little toes were decorated with tattoos. Sara had never seen anything like this before and she was amazed. When she looked up again, she noticed that Mrs. Sunburn was wearing about a dozen silver chains around her neck, and on each chain dangled a silver heart or flower. Ah, how sweet. Sara mused.

Is that a monk? Sara suddenly thought.

Standing beside her was a girl—at least she thought it was a girl. The monk's features were very fine and delicate, her head was shaved bald, and she was wearing a thick brown floor-length burlap robe with wide billowing sleeves. Sitting on top of the girl's head was a small brown opaque tight-fitting brimless cap. Sara tried to see what the monk was wearing on her feet, but was unable to locate her feet beneath the heavy robe. *I've never seen a real live monk before, but I imagine this is how one would look,* she thought.

The hefty, brown skinned couple dressed in black received their order and moved on down the line. The line-up started moving again, and eventually it was Sara's turn to place her order, and so she did. After paying, the salesgirl, Sara loaded her food on a tray and made her way to join Meaghan and the children.

"Sorry that took so long," Sara apologized.

"It's not your fault, Sara, its swamped in here! We're people watching," Meaghan replied.

"Aren't airports the most interesting places? Filled with all kinds of characters, all of us different, and yet we're all at the same place at the same time."

"People are very fascinating!" Sara said. "I think I just saw a monk—did you see her Meaghan?"

"I don't think we saw anyone that looked like a monk, did either of you see a monk?" Meaghan asked her children.

"What's a monk?" Tara asked.

"I wanna see a monkey," Cohen chimed in.

Sara and Meaghan burst out laughing at the same time, and Megan said, "Out of the mouths of babes."

"I don't think there are any monkeys here in the airport, at least not the four-legged, furry kind you're looking for, Cohen," Sara informed him with a chuckle.

Meaghan pointed to a lady with very straight posture sitting at a table near a window and quietly said, "Did you notice that lady over there when she was placing her order?" The lady's very bright red hair with very gray one-inch roots was piled on top of her head. Sitting at the table with her were three younger versions of herself with the same very red hair, minus the very gray roots, but with the same very ramrod-straight posture.

"What did she do?" Sara asked, biting into her warm buttered cranberry scone.

Meaghan replied, "She placed an order for one glazed scone. When she got the order she asked for one more glazed scone. When she got that one, she ordered one more glazed scone. She did that four times. Don't you think she could have said, 'I'd like four glazed scones, please?'

"That sounds reasonable to me," Sara replied with a chuckle. "Sometimes people do some very strange things."

Sara, Meaghan, and the children continued eating their breakfast, watching the people around them and enjoying the show. "Thanks for breakfast, Sara, we were all pretty hungry, and it tasted really good," Meaghan told her with a warm smile.

"Oh, you're very welcome, Meaghan, this has been a great way to start our day. We should land in Vancouver at 12:30," Sara replied. "If we're all finished our breakfast lets move on to find our boarding gate and let someone else have this table."

The foursome proceeded to their desired destination, and sat down on the bright orange airport seats.

"I think Enlighten will send someone to pick us up at the airport and take us to our hotel room in Vancouver, does that sound right to you, Sara?" Meaghan asked.

"Yes, I believe so, Meaghan. Oh, I know what I forgot to tell you—my son Luc will be flying our airplane to Vancouver today," Sara said in a matter-of-fact tone.

Meaghan looked at Sara as if she had just said she was growing horns. "You're *what* is doing *what?*" Meaghan asked in horror. "I hope he's a pilot!"

"*Of course* he is—sorry; I forgot to mention that to you. My son has been a commercial airline pilot for Canada Airlines for a few years now, and he's going to be flying our plane to Vancouver today."

"Is there a reason why you never told me this before today?" Meaghan asked.

"I guess it never came up. He flies daily from Saskatoon to Vancouver and back again. Sometimes he gets layovers in Vancouver, so we should see quite a bit of him while we're there."

"Sara, I'm stunned at this news! Are you sure the children and I won't be a burden to you if you and your son want to go out and do things together? What did you say his name is—Lucas?"

"His name is Luc, and if he is around when I have Tara and Cohen, we'll just take your children along with us wherever we go. He loves kids; it'll all work out fine. So please, don't worry!"

Meaghan *was* worried; her brow was creased, and her lips were pursed together when a very tall, dark and handsome airline pilot walked up to them. He stooped down and planted a kiss on his mother's forehead.

"Well, look who's here! Could this be my gorgeous mother?" Luc asked as he grinned at Sara.

"Luc, what a nice surprise, we were just talking about you."

Sara stood up and gave her son a big kiss and a warm hug. "It's great to see you, son. How are you?"

"I'm fine, mother, thanks—and who have we got here?" He said as Cohen and Tara pressed in close around him.

"Luc, this is my friend, Meaghan, the one I told you I'm going on the Enlighten tour with. And these are her two children, Princess Tara, who is five years old and Cohen, the mighty dragon slayer, who is two."

"I don't think I've ever had the honor of actually shaking hands with a princess or a dragon slayer before. This is a very special day," Luc said solemnly as he shook hands with Tara and Cohen. "And I know for sure I've never shaken hands with a beautiful queen mother before. I'm honored to meet you, your Royal Highness," Luc said with a bow while shaking Meaghan's hand.

Meaghan and the children couldn't help but let out a little giggle. Then she said, "It's an honor to meet you, Captain Luc. The children and I have never had the opportunity to shake hands with a real live airline pilot before either, isn't that right, kids?"

Tara and Cohen both nodded their heads in quiet agreement. They were completely awestruck with Luc's size and uniform, and were at a loss for words, which was a totally new sensation for either of them.

"Well very nice to meet all you royal people, and great to see you, Mom. You look very nice, by the way," Luc said, glancing at his watch. "I must leave. It's time to go fly an airplane." Luc raised his hand to his hat and saluted the children. Then he walked away.

"Is he a really pilot—is he gonna fly a airplane?" Cohen asked.

"How did he get to be a real pilot?" Tara asked.

"Yes and yes. He is a real pilot, Cohen. He is going to fly us to Vancouver, and Tara, you'll have to ask Luc about how he got to be a real pilot. I know that he went to school for a long time and he took flying lessons," Sara responded, laughing at the children's admiration of her son.

Sara and Meaghan started gathering up their travel bags. "Luc has sad eyes," Meaghan said. "His voice sounds happy, but he's sad inside."

Sara looked at Meaghan. "You are very observant young lady, but you'll have to talk to Luc about that.

Now, come along everyone. I hear them calling us to get on the airplane."

"Just a minute, Sara—before we go, let's say a prayer. We need to pray for safe travel, and also that God will bless our adventure—and let's pray for Luc. I don't know what he's going through, but let's pray that he'll find peace and happiness."

With that being said, Megan broke into prayer. "Our Heavenly Father, we ask You to keep us safe on this flight to Vancouver and bless us all on our new adventure, and give Luc the wisdom and skill he needs to fly our plane. And we pray that Luc will find peace of mind in You, Lord, thank You, in Jesus.' Amen."

After the prayer, the foursome formed a line which proceeded onto the plane where they found their seats, all in the same row. Tara was by the window, then Meaghan, and next to her sat Cohen, with Sara by the aisle. In no time at all, they were buckled in.

The airline hostess gave her safety spiel, and they were taxiing down the runway. Soon they were flying west across the clear blue sky.

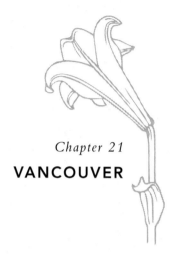

Chapter 21
VANCOUVER

The flight from Saskatoon to Vancouver took place uneventfully. As much as Cohen fought the idea of taking a nap, he did finally succumb, and fell asleep looking like a little angel with his tired two-year-old tousled head resting peacefully on his super-hero coloring book. Tara sat quietly coloring pictures of princesses the whole way to Vancouver, occasionally stopping her coloring to glue and sprinkle sparkles on the pages, which made the princesses appear very glamorous.

Sara utilized her flying time by delving into a best-selling novel she'd been waiting to read, while Megan nervously leafed through some fashion magazines. Meaghan appeared calm and cool on the exterior, but inside she was a bundle of nerves.

Upon disembarking from the flight, the little entourage collected their luggage and headed for the exit. Meaghan began counting, "one, two, and three."

Looking around, she asked no one in particular. "Do we have all the bags?"

"Meaghan, look over there," Sara said, pointing to a tall thin man with a gorgeous head of thick black curly hair. He was holding up a sign that read, "Welcome Meaghan Marshall!" Standing very close to him stood a flamboyantly-dressed middle-aged woman.

"Come children," Meaghan said, and she and Sara and the children headed in their direction.

"You must be Meaghan!" the stranger exclaimed. Meaghan's eyes traveled over to the lady at his side who was dressed in a flamingo dancer costume. Her dazzling skirt consisted of layer upon layer of bright red sparkling fabric with silver rickrack edging each layer. Her shimmering white off-the-shoulder shirt was tucked into the waistline, accenting her very tiny waist. Shoulder-length thick black curly hair framed her beautifully-painted face, and behind her right ear was tucked a blood-red rose.

"Are you a gypsy?" Tara asked the lady.

"Tara, shush," Meaghan scolded her quietly.

"Oh, that's okay," the lady answered. "I *am* a gypsy, and I love being one. Are you a princess?" she asked Tara.

"How did you know that?" Tara asked back in surprise.

"Well, that's easy to tell—you look like a princess should look," the gypsy replied.

Tara stood back, amazed by the lady's wisdom. She couldn't take her eyes off the gypsy's beauty and her amazing costume.

The tall, thin man stepped forward and began making introductions. "Welcome to Vancouver, Ms. Marshall," he said, reaching out his hand to shake Meaghan's. "My name is Benjamin Balduci, but you can call me Benny. I'm filling in for Laura today to welcome you and get you settled into your hotel. On behalf of the Enlighten Weight Loss Company, I would like to extend our deepest gratitude to you for taking on the role of Ambassador for the Enlighten Company. We very sincerely promise to be here for you and make your journey as pleasant as possible."

"Meaghan, this is my assistant, Thelma Frapacini" he continued. "She is my right-hand woman, so to speak, and she will be your attendant daily. Her job is to assist you in applying your makeup, and selecting the appropriate wardrobe— as you can see, she definitely has an eye for style!"

"Thank you, Benjamin—I mean Benny. But how did you possibly know who I was?" Meaghan asked.

"Ah," Benny said. "I happen to have this photograph of a very beautiful, dark-haired young woman with sparkling green eyes, lovely to look at, with a slender figure and long shapely legs. I'd say she looks a lot like you." He held up the picture comparing it to Meaghan.

Of course, Meaghan thought, *a picture.* She was very humbled by his kind words; she was not used to such extravagant compliments. "Benny and Thelma, I'd like you to meet my dear friend and my children's nanny, Sara. She's the one who made this whole trip possible by volunteering her services for child care for Tara and Cohen." Meaghan said, placing her hand on each child as she mentioned their names. Meaghan continued. "As I'm sure you're aware, they'll all be coming on tour with me. You probably know as much as or more about the details of this trip than I do. But we're all thoroughly thrilled about this adventure! I'm just wondering, will we have time to sit down later and go through the itinerary and my job description? I really need to know what your expectations are."

Benny and Thelma reached out and began shaking hands with Sara and the children. "We're very pleased to meet you," Benny said, and Thelma nodded agreement. "In answer to your question, Meaghan, there is a small dinner/get-together planned for later this evening to discuss any concerns you might have," When Benny smiled, a deep dimple appeared in each of his cheeks, making him appear remarkably handsome. Then he continued. "But for now, let's find someone to take care of these bags, and then we'll get you all over to your hotel. There should be a little time for you to take a rest and regroup before we meet again." Once again, he flashed his dimpled smile at Meaghan.

"That sounds wonderful," Meaghan responded, beginning to relax and feel more at ease.

Benny tipped the concierge to take care of their bags, but Cohen insisted on pushing his own wheeled superhero backpack himself. "Watch where you're going, Cohen!" his mother warned, as he seemed to be more fascinated by the way the backpack moved rather than where he was walking.

"My mini-van is ready and waiting for us," Benny informed them.

"You lead the way!" Meaghan responded.

The little entourage headed towards the exit sign and was ready to exit when they heard a loud shout from behind.

"Sara, Meaghan! Wait up!"

The little group swiveled around simultaneously to see Luc hurrying towards them. His cheeks were flushed, and his airline-issued neck tie was flying askew as he hurried to catch up to them, but other than that, he looked as polished and professional as he had before the flight.

"Luc!" Cohen shouted, dropping his backpack; he barreled over to throw himself into Luc's long legs. Luc was quick to react, and neatly caught Cohen up in his arms, swooping him high into the air and then setting him gently back down on his feet. "Whoa, there young man, you are a fast runner. Who taught you how to run so fast, your sister?" Luc asked.

"I run fastr'n Tara," Cohen proclaimed earnestly.

"You can not run faster than me, Cohen. I just let you win sometimes," Tara put in indignantly.

Then with a total change of attitude, she looked up at Luc, smiled sweetly, batted her eyelashes, and asked coyly, "Are you coming to the hotel with us?"

"Who is this child, and where did she come from?" Meahgan exclaimed.

"I can stay at your hotel, I guess; I have to stay somewhere. I was hoping we could all go out together later for dinner," he said, looking at his mother.

Sara was beaming at the sight of her son. She reached out and put her hand on Luc's arm and said. "This is a real treat seeing you again, son. I believe that Meaghan has a previous engagement, but the children and I would love to have dinner with you! Wouldn't we, children?"

"Well, let's make it a foursome then, you and Tara, and me and Cohen," Luc said. "What do you think of that idea?" Luc asked as he ruffled Cohen's hair and winked at Tara.

"I'm sure the children would love that, wouldn't you?" Meaghan asked them.

Tara and Cohen jumped up and down and let out a loud, "YEAH!"

Cohen was hanging onto Luc's hand and Tara continued, "We get to eat dinner with a real live pilot."

"Our rooms are at the Ritz Renaissance," Sara informed her son.

"Well, why don't I stay there too, then?" Luc replied, a big smile spreading across his face.

"YEAH!" Cohen yelled again, pulling on Luc's hand and skipping along beside him, totally forgetting about his wheeled backpack as they once again started towards the door.

Luc looked down at the energetic little boy that was hanging onto him, and his handsome face lit up in a big grin. He hadn't felt this happy in a long time.

Tara hurried over to Luc's other side and walked quietly along beside him. She thought it might be okay to share her little brother with this big man, but she didn't want to be left out. *After all, I am the oldest and I need to watch out for him, he's just a baby,* she thought.

Sara introduced her son to Benny and Thelma. Then, grabbing up Cohen's abandoned backpack, they all made their way to Benny's mini-van.

"Maybe I should call a taxi," Luc suggested.

"I think there's enough room for everyone," Benny said. With a little squeezing and much giggling and teasing, they did all fit quite snugly into the vehicle. Benjamin and Thelma sat in the front seat. Sara, Meaghan and Tara in the second row, and Luc and Cohen crawled way in the back. Meaghan had quickly installed the children's booster car seats, and soon they were on their way to the Ritz Renaissance. The luggage all managed to fit neatly in the roof-top carrier. From the angle Luc was sitting, he caught a glimpse of Meaghan's profile, and did a double-take.

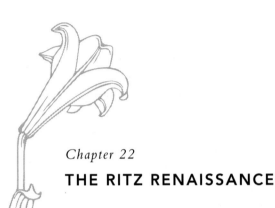

Chapter 22

THE RITZ RENAISSANCE

I believe she's the most beautiful woman I've ever seen, and she's totally unaware of it! Luc thought. *That is a very appealing quality.*

Benny made his way carefully through the traffic to the Ritz Renaissance Hotel. Once there, he parked in front of the main doors and announced, "We're here, everybody out."

They all took their turns climbing out of the van. Sara laughingly did a little moaning about the kinks in her legs, and began shaking them out. Soon they were all standing on solid ground, and Luc helped Benny unload the luggage.

A bellhop suddenly appeared and stowed the bags on a wheeled trolley. Benny and Thelma made plans to meet up with Meaghan later, and then drove away.

The attentive bellhop escorted the little group into the hotel lobby, and they checked in. Enlighten had reserved a suite for Meaghan and her children with an adjoining room for Sara. Luc booked a single room for himself across the hall on the same floor.

"Well, the children and I are off to our room to relax and unwind for awhile," Meaghan announced with a smile. "I'm supposed to meet with the Enlighten members in the Paradise Ballroom at five o'clock." Turning her attention to the bellhop, she asked, "Please tell me, where exactly is the Paradise Ballroom?"

The bellhop gave Meaghan the required directions. "What about us?" Luc asked. "Where and when should we meet, Mom?"

"Let's meet at five o'clock, too," Sara answered. "Come over to my room then and we can decide where we'll go for supper, is that okay?"

"That sounds good to me," Luc said. "You two try to stay out of trouble, and let your mother have some rest." He tousled Cohen's hair.

On that note everyone disappeared into their respective rooms.

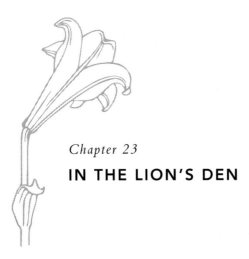

Chapter 23

IN THE LION'S DEN

Once inside their hotel room, Meaghan instructed her children to stretch out on the floor, and relax while she unpacked. She turned the television on to a cartoon channel and tossed them each a throw cushion from the couch. "Here you go; I'm going to a take a nice long soak in the bathtub. Is there anything I can get you before I do?"

"I need a drink please, Mom, I'm thirsty," Tara stated.

"Me too, drink milk," Cohen chimed in.

"Okay, I'll see if there's any milk in the refrigerator," Meaghan replied.

The refrigerator had been fully stocked for them, and Meaghan was impressed. She found an unopened liter of two-percent milk, and poured two glasses each half full. Setting them on the coffee table beside her children, she said, "Here you go. Now please be good and no fighting! I'm going to be in the bathtub for a long time."

The children were already zoned out to reality and focused on watching a little round red tomato and a long green English cucumber singing and dancing.

Meaghan ran a tub full of steaming hot water. She generously sprinkled in some lovely fragrant lavender bath salts, quickly undressed, pinned her long black hair up on top of her head, and carefully stepped into the heavenly-smelling water. Slowly lowering her body into the tub, she laid her head back on a deliciously soft bathtub pillow and relaxed, letting out a long sigh.

Down the hall, Luc paced the floor of his hotel room. His mind wouldn't let him relax and stop thinking about Meaghan. *How come she has to be so darn gorgeous?* He thought. "And what can I do about it, Lord?" he asked out loud. "I need to find out what's going on with, Lisa. God, You know I've been trying to find her. Where is she? I need Your help, Lord—am I free to move on, or do I wait? Jesus, help me!"

I'm praying, how about that? I haven't prayed for a long time. I wonder if God will actually hear me. It is comforting, though, Luc thought.

At five o'clock, Sara was in her room when she heard a short knock on the door. She hurried over to open the door and there stood her son, Luc.

"Hello, Mom." he said. He walked over to her and gave his mother a big hug. "Once again, you look wonderful. Is that a new outfit?"

"Of course it is. You didn't think I would go on a Canada-wide tour without getting myself some new clothes, did you?"

"Honestly mom, I never actually thought about this whole Canada-wide tour until I saw you ready to board the plane yesterday. I think it's great for you, though. I'm glad you decided to do it."

"Your gladness about this wouldn't be because you get to spend time with my gorgeous young friend and her two adorable children, would it?" Sara asked teasingly.

Luc tilted his head to the side and scrutinized his mother. "You're very perceptive for a mother, and how do you feel about that?"

"My advice is to go slow, Luc. Meaghan and her children are very vulnerable and you have some issues to straighten out, too. Try to not rush into anything, just take your time."

"Thanks, Mom, for the advice, I will try to heed it," Luc told his mother with a smile.

There was a light knock on the door adjoining the two rooms, and in stepped Meaghan, with Tara and Cohen in tow. Upon seeing Luc standing with Sara, the children rushed excitedly over to hug him.

Meaghan looked her usual breathtaking self, dressed for dinner in a long flowing apple-green silky skirt. The peasant-style blouse she wore to accompany it was in a creamy-colored silk and had long flowing sleeves. Draped loosely around her shoulders was a light, airy mohair wrap in a deep shade of raspberry. Meaghan's thick black hair hung soft and loose around her bare shoulders and behind her right ear was a delicate deep pink peony, matching the color of her wrap. Her bare sun-tanned feet were strapped into two-inch spike-heeled silver sandals, showing off French-manicured toenails.

Luc's eyes landed on Meaghan's tiny toes and traveled all the way up to the top of her head. "Wow!" he exclaimed under his breath. "You look like an exquisite flower."

Meaghan's eyes met Luc's. She flushed under his scrutiny, and turned her eyes away. At that moment, Benny and Thelma walked up to the open doorway. "Hello everyone, how nice to see you all again and looking absolutely gorgeous, I might add." Benny said glancing around the group.

"And back at you," Meaghan responded warmly.

"What adventure do the four of you have planned for this evening?" Benny asked, glancing around from Luc to the children once again showing off his charming dimples.

"We haven't had a chance to discuss that yet. What are you two hungry for?" Luc asked, directing his gaze at Tara and Cohen.

"Pizza!" Cohen shouted.

"What about you Tara, what would you like?" Luc asked.

"Pizza's fine," she replied. "I also like French fries and cheese burgers and chicken strips and spaghetti and most salads," she replied solemnly.

"A and double doo?" Cohen announced, jumping up and down.

Luc laughed and said. "I don't think we'll go to A and double doo tonight, buddy. Maybe we'll go there next time. I know a great restaurant, not far from here, that serves everything you like—pizza and fries and cheese burgers and chicken strips, and salads. Should we try that one tonight? Is that okay with you, Mom?"

"That sounds wonderful to me, Luc, let's go," Sara responded.

"Oh, just one minute, before you leave—Sara, will you be okay when you get back from dinner? Do you know where to find the kid's pyjamas and get them ready for bed?" Meaghan asked.

"Yes, I can manage that, Meaghan; I checked out their room while you were soaking in the tub, and I'm sure they can help me if there's anything we can't find. After we get back from our meal, I'll take Tara and Cohen back to your room, bathe them and then get them ready for bed."

"That sounds perfect, Sara, thanks," Meaghan said. She raised her hand in a farewell salute. Looking at her children, she said, "Okay, you guys have fun, and remember your manners!"

"We will, Mom," Tara replied.

"See you later, Cohen," Meaghan said as she started walking away with Benny and Thelma.

"Later, Mom, you have fun, member manners," Cohen solemnly repeated to his mother.

Meaghan let out a little chuckle and headed off with her two companions.

"Let's go, tigers!" Luc said, grabbing Cohen's hand on one side and Tara's on the other. He grinned at his mother. "Come on, Gramma. We're off to find us some food and adventure."

Luc and his entourage walked down the street to a nearby restaurant for their dinner. It was called the Lion's Den, and there were two huge stuffed lions inside guarding the entrance. In the middle of the dining room was a gigantic sunken fish pond teeming with humungous gold fish. The fish seemed to be about the same size as a Pickerel or a Perch.

Placed in strategic spots throughout the den were other very authentic-looking stuffed lions. One life-sized mother lion was lying on a six-foot-high man-made cliff, sunning herself with four little lion kittens nursing at her breasts. Another tawny-colored lion was crouched on the limb of an old oak tree, right over their heads, as if it was ready to pounce. It looked so real that Cohen decided to keep his eye on it, just in case it moved.

Each of the four walls was covered from floor to ceiling with movie screens showing slide shows of animal safaris. It gave the perception that the safari jeeps were traveling right through the restaurant, an excellent way to keep young patrons entertained while they waited for their food. The waiters were dressed in authentic-looking African safari hunting attire. Luc, Sara and the children placed their order with their waiter, and then Luc took his two little charges on a tour around the room. Cohen and Tara were amazed at their surroundings.

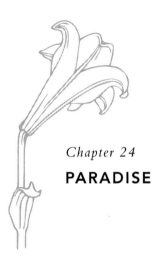

Chapter 24

PARADISE

Meaghan and her two escorts made their way down the hall to the Paradise Ballroom. As the three entered the ornately-decorated room, Meaghan felt many eyes turning to stare at them.

The president and the members of the Enlighten Weight Loss Program had been watching for Meaghan, and hurried over to greet her.

"Welcome Meaghan and Benny and Thelma," The president said warmly, my name is Cassandra. She introduced Meaghan to the other Enlighten members and then asked Meaghan a few questions about herself. In no time at all, the ice was broken, and Meaghan began to feel at ease.

"Later we'll get together and discuss some of what your position as ambassador for this program entails, but for now, let's just relax and enjoy. Isn't this a beautiful room?" the president asked.

"It certainly is," Meaghan replied "I can't believe this is really happening. Now that I'm actually here, I feel like I'm ready to slow down and enjoy the moment. I'm primed to talk business with you whenever you're ready." Meaghan smiled, and reaching out, she took a small glass of sparkling red wine from the server, and then strolled over to check out a bubbling brook running through Paradise. Benny and Thelma recognized someone from across the room and walked over to greet them.

The guests, which Meaghan learned consisted mostly of sponsors for the program, some Enlighten board members and city dignitaries, interacted for half an hour while a lone guitar player perched on a tall bar stool quietly strummed his guitar, entertaining them with love ballads.

During the meal, Meaghan sat beside Benny who sat next to Thelma. *How cute are these two—one of them doesn't seem to go anywhere without the other one,* Meaghan thought.

The main course consisted of fresh pecan-crusted tilapia in a very tasty sauce. It was served over rice pilaf accompanied by a delicious garden salad. The lime sherbet dessert was presented in tall, elegant crystal glasses. Meaghan loved the tangy refreshing zip of the sherbet.

After the meal was completed, Meaghan met with the head office officials to discuss her contract and the traveling plans. They were gathered together in an office next door to the ballroom, and asked Meaghan if she would like someone to sit in with her as her representative. Meaghan couldn't really think of anyone to ask, so she declined the offer.

"We will be your team throughout this tour; remember that we're on your side. We want you to succeed as well as have a very pleasant experience. If there's anything you need, or if you have problems of any kind, please don't forget that we are just a phone call away. The tour is not heavily scheduled, but it's steady. We expect you to get plenty of rest; participate in the exercise regimes planned into your schedule—try your best to stay healthy and always looking your best."

"We're thrilled that your children could come with you. I'm sure you will be much more relaxed." the president said. "And also, I believe that the mother/children image will help present our weight-loss program as a plan that works for the average woman, not some super model."

"I'm very thankful that you've allowed my children to come on this tour with me. I know I couldn't have done the tour without them," Meaghan replied.

Meaghan and the group discussed more details of the trip: her wardrobe, makeup, and hair care would all be supplied by the company while she was on tour. Her entire expenses would be absorbed by the company, and when the tour was completed, she would get a lump sum salary of one hundred thousand dollars. Meaghan was thrilled. She signed the contract. "Well, if that's all for tonight, and if I have to look my best for tomorrow, I'd better get some sleep," Meaghan stated.

"Yes of course, that's it for tonight; you make a beautiful Ambassador for Enlighten, and I thank you again for taking on this tour. Goodnight, Meaghan," the president said, shaking Meaghan's hand. She then continued: "I believe you will be a real asset to our program, Meaghan, but just one more thing before you leave us tonight. Have you heard from Anna Baldman, the former representative? Do you know how she's doing?"

"Sara did go to visit her before the tour started, and apparently she has had surgery and is now undergoing radiation treatments. She was in good health prior to this and she has a positive attitude, so we're just really praying that she will have a full recovery."

"Well, that's good news, Meaghan. We too hope that she'll be fine," Cassandra replied.

Meaghan thanked the President and board for their support, and agreed that she would do her very best to be a positive role model for their company. On her way out of the door, she turned, smiled, and said, "Breakfast back in this room tomorrow at eight o'clock, right?"

"Yes, we'll meet here for breakfast tomorrow, and it will be your first official day of work. After breakfast, we'll get your measurements taken, and the wardrobe personnel will kick into gear assembling your outfits for the first week of your tour. The hair and makeup people will also be available to experiment on colours and styles for you. Tomorrow will be a big day!" the President stated.

"Oh, I'm so excited; I can't wait to get started!" Meaghan trilled.

"See you in the morning then, have a good night." one of the board members told her.

Meaghan hugged Benny and then Thelma. She shook hands with Cassandra, and other board members and left the room.

Meaghan floated upstairs as if on a cloud. She felt elated, and couldn't remember the last time she'd been this happy. Upon reaching her room, she quietly slipped her key card into the door slot, and upon opening the door she noticed Sara dressed in a soft aqua bathrobe, reclining on the sofa and leafing through a magazine. Luc, still dressed in his street clothes, was perched on a bar stool at the counter scanning his laptop. "Well, our Cinderella is home. Do you still have both glass slippers on?" Luc asked.

"I feel like Cinderella,' Meaghan replied. "Can this actually be happening to little ole me? It's a dream come true that I never even knew I was dreaming."

"You deserve it, my friend," Sara responded, walking over and enfolding Meaghan in her arms. "Tell us all about your evening." Sara said, wanting to know every detail.

Meaghan sat down on the sofa, curling her legs under her. "Okay, I will. But first, tell me how you made out with Cohen and Tara. Did they give you any grief?" she asked.

"Are you kidding me?" Sara replied. "They are little angels. When we got back here after dinner, they wanted Luc and I to play house with them, so we did.

Big surprise, I was to play the part of Gramma, Tara was the mom, Cohen was the dad, and Luc was the little boy. How's that for role reversal? Apparently there was also a medium-sized, black and white dog in the family, but Luc and I couldn't see him."

"Oh, that Cohen cracks me up!" Luc cut in, chuck-ling. "He told me that I was the little boy and my name was 'house pet.' But now listen to this: the dog's name was 'house pet' too! I had the same name as the dog. Playing with them was so much fun; it made Mom and me feel like kids again. They have great imaginations, and they play together very well."

"I'm glad to hear that." Meaghan said, letting out a little cackle.

"We put them to bed about eight o'clock." Sara said, "And were out like lights once their heads hit their pillows. They must have been exhausted—speaking of which, so am I, Meaghan. Tell me about your wonderful evening, and then I'm going to head for my room and my bed."

Meaghan filled Sara and Luc in on the events of her evening. She told them about the beautiful Paradise Ballroom, about the meal, and finally the contract.

"Are you happy with the terms of the contract, or do you think we should get a lawyer to take a look at it?" Sara asked.

"Oh no, I trust them completely. They're not going to take advantage of me; they assured me that we are all on the same team," Meaghan reassured her friend.

"Well, if you're happy, I'm happy. Now, you two young people can burn the midnight candle if you want, but I'm bushed. What are your plans for tomorrow, Luc? Will you have some time to hang out with me and the kids?"

"I don't have any plans for tomorrow, Mom, and I think I can handle one more day with you and the kids. I suppose Enlighten has a full day planned for you, Meaghan?"

"Oh, yes!" Meaghan said with a smile. "My job begins tomorrow—I'm officially going to start wowing the country. Breakfast starts at eight o'clock, and then we plan wardrobe, hairstyles etc. I think I'll be busy until at least four. But before you go, Sara, have you heard any news about Anna? That's the one thing about this position that troubles me. I know I got the job by default. Do you know how she's doing?"

Sara replied, "It's been at least a week since I phoned her. She'd had all her radiation treatments and now plays the waiting game for six weeks. Then the doctor will check to see if the treatments were effective. She told me that she was feeling pretty good, just a little weak; she said that food didn't have any taste, so naturally she's lost a lot of weight. We must remember to pray for her recovery, but she did ask about you, Meaghan. She was thrilled that you were going ahead with this tour, and was very excited to hear that I was going along to look after your children. She said to keep her in the loop."

"Thanks Sara, that sounds fairly positive. The team asked me about her tonight and I wasn't sure how she was doing. I will certainly try to remember to pray for a complete recovery for her," Meaghan said.

"Good for you Meaghan, goodnight, you two—Luc, do you want to stay overnight in my room? There is an extra bed," Sara asked.

"Thanks, Mom, but I have a room just down the hall. Don't worry; I'll be back here in the morning to harass you and the kids." Luc walked over and gave his Mom a gentle hug and a kiss on the cheek.

"See you tomorrow, then," Sara said, giving her son a warm smile.

"Thanks for today, Sara," Meaghan said.

"You are quite welcome. See you tomorrow morning, and sleep tight, Meaghan," Sara told her friend and left.

"Well, guess I should be on my way home too, it's almost ten o'clock. You've had a long day, and it will be another busy day tomorrow. I just want to thank you, Meaghan, and tell you how appreciative I am that you trust my Mom and me with your kids. I think this might be just what Mom needs to get her back on track. She's been in kind of a slump since Dad died, and on the selfish side of things, I think this will be good for me, too. Did my mother tell you about my relationship with a woman that went sour?" Luc asked.

"She only mentioned that you were going through a broken relationship, but she didn't give me any details," Meaghan quickly replied.

"My last relationship has turned into a nightmare that I don't know how to deal with. I have decided to leave it in God's hands; He'll tell me what to do. But right now I think your family will be the best therapy for my mother and me, so thanks again, Meaghan."

"You're very welcome, Luc—I never thought of myself as providing therapy for anyone. You know, obviously, that my marriage to the children's father didn't work out, or I wouldn't be here. Sometimes things happen beyond our control, and we just have to try and hold ourselves together until eventually we can make the effort to start over again. I think it must be like a grieving process—we lose someone we love, and it takes time to get over them. It takes a lot of strength and courage, but I'm ready now. I believe that this job will be good for me and the children. It's like I get to start all over again and I'm ready!"

"Good for you, Meaghan! I've just met you, but from what I've seen so far, it looks like you're choosing to bloom right where you've been planted. You certainly take good care of your children, and seem to have a lot of common sense, just like my Mom. Now I'm going to say goodnight and let you get your beauty sleep. I have great admiration for you—you're not letting the past get you down. I think I can learn a lot from you."

Luc walked over to Meaghan; she stood up and they hugged. He kissed her on the forehead and said goodnight.

"Good night Luc, sleep well," Meaghan replied.

THE END.